Right Hand Man

by

Paula F. Winskye

This book is a work of fiction. Events and situations in this story are purely fictional. Any resemblance to persons, living or dead, is coincidental.

ISBN: 978-1502317155

Prolog

"How could you be so stupid!"

Karlea Johnson cringed while her husband Bill ranted. She knew that he would never strike her. But his words had a way of hurting more than a fist.

She spoke in a small voice. "I thought it would look good on you."

"How long have we been married! Fourteen years! Have you ever known me to wear yellow?"

"No. I'll take it back."

"You're damned right you will! And don't ever pull a bonehead move like that again." He threw his cigarette to the concrete and crushed it with his boot. "And now I've had to waste my time coming out here to tell you what you already knew. I should be in the field. I expected this of you when you were a teenaged bride. There's no excuse for this. Get back to work."

Karlea bit her lip as he stalked from the barn. She picked up a saddle, then set it down. When she heard his pickup roar out of the yard, she covered her face and began sobbing.

A hand touched her shoulder. Karlea spun to face her 17-year-old hired man, Cody Pfeiffer.

"Y-you h-heard?"

"Yeah."

"I'm sorry."

"You're not the one who needs to apologize. He shouldn't treat you like that."

"I screwed up."

"You bought him a yellow shirt because you thought it'd look good on him. Geez, Karlea, he threw a fit. I mean, that would've been overreacting even if you'd gambled away $10,000."

"I should have known better. I should've known he'd be mad. It's my own fault."

"You don't deserve to be treated like that. You're a nice lady, Karlea. You were just trying to be nice. If he really didn't want the shirt, all he had to do was say so. He knows you're not stupid. He shouldn't call you names."

"Oh, thank you, Cody. You're such a sweet boy. Hiring you was the nicest thing he's ever done for me." She wiped her eyes. "Would it make you really uncomfortable if I asked for a hug?"

"No. Ask anytime."

He hugged her for as long as she wanted. She stepped back, her emotions under control.

"Thank you. I may ask again. Though Bill would have a fit if he ever saw us."

"What Bill doesn't know won't hurt him."

"You're a terrific kid. And you work so hard."

Cody blushed. "Quit that. I'll get a big head. I figure I'd better work hard. If I want to work with horses, this is the only job around."

"You can work for me as long as you like. And, remember, if you decide to go to horseshoing school, I'll talk Bill into helping you with tuition."

"How'll you do that?"

"Bill knows what I pay the farrier. I'll make him see the wisdom of investing in your future."

I

Horizontal snow. Karlea sighed in her warm kitchen, staring out at the heavy, wet snow, driven by a 40 mile-per-hour northwest wind. The meteorologists called it an Alberta clipper.

"God, this is a bad April Fool's Day joke."

Yesterday, she and Cody had been forced to shed their sweatshirts.

She strained her eyes through the snow, searching for him. An hour ago he had ridden out to bring in the broodmares. She had watched them drift into the corral over the past few minutes. But they would be inside if he were with them.

"Where are you, Cody?"

I can't wait any longer. If he's hurt, this weather can kill even a rugged 23-year old. Karlea bundled up before stepping outside. The wind caught the storm door, almost ripping it from her hands. She forced it shut and negotiated the icy steps. Though the temperature hovered near thirty, the wind chill ran closer to zero. She plodded against the clipper, staying on the grass. The rain, which had preceded the snow, rendered any smooth surface treacherous.

Fear grabbed her stomach when she saw Cody's big pinto gelding, Dan, standing off by himself.

"Oh, no. Cody. God, please let him be okay."

She worked her way through the mares. Seeing Dan's reins tied to the saddle horn, she let her breath out. Cody had sent him back. *One of the mares must have foaled in this storm.*

She wiped snow off the saddle before mounting. But the wet leather soaked her jeans, further chilling her. Her feet came nowhere near Cody's stirrups, making it difficult to keep her knee-high rubber boots on.

She urged the reluctant gelding along the trail of muddy hoofprints, hoping that Cody had found the mare with the herd. *If I have to search the whole pasture, I may not find him in time.*

When she crested the hill protecting the ranch, the full force of the blizzard hit her. She thanked God that she did not have to travel directly into the wind. Keeping her eyes on the ground, she pushed Dan on.

There! A single set of tracks from the east joined the others. Karlea stopped for a closer look. *Horse shoes!* Only Dan wore shoes. Asking for more speed, she back-tracked the trail.

Over the next rise she almost ran into Cody, lugging a wet foal. Duchess kept her nose near her baby. When the mare saw Dan, her ears flattened.

Karlea reined away in time to avoid her charge, but Duchess sent Cody and the foal sprawling on the wet ground. Always a good mother, she returned to the foal, nuzzled it, then Cody as he picked himself up. He glared at Karlea, who scolded herself.

How could I be so stupid?

"Go put Dan and the mares in! I'll bring these two!"

Karlea nodded, wheeled Dan, and cantered toward the barn. She kept to the ridges for better footing as long as she could. Dismounting outside the corral, she left him and threaded her way through the mares.

When she opened the door, they spilled into the barn. She followed; closing stalls as soon as they were occupied, barking commands if two mares entered the same stall.

When she confined the last mare, she noticed Dan standing in the doorway. He knew better than to enter with mares loose. She opened his stall. "Come, Dan."

Without waiting, she collected supplies, opened a foaling stall, and turned on the radiant heater. She heard Dan's hooves on the concrete aisle and hurried to unsaddle him. While closing his stall door, she saw Cody approaching the corral.

"Thank God."

He struggled through the mud, finally placing the foal on its wobbly legs inside the barn. He leaned against the wall shivering, exhausted.

"You're soaked. Go get those wet clothes off. I can take it from here."

He nodded as she closed the barn door. She guided the baby to the stall with Duchess following. Karlea put her muscles into drying the baby, a girl, then treated her navel with iodine.

When the filly began searching for a meal, Karlea left the stall. Cody had not moved.

"Cody! You need to get to the house!"

Glassy eyes stared at her. He had stopped shivering. *Hypothermia. I don't have much time.* She prodded him along the aisle to a door closer to the house.

"Don't fall. I'll never get you up."

Only constant urging kept him moving. Once outside, the barn provided shelter for a few yards, then the wind pushed them along. When he reached the steps, he stumbled, but somehow landed on his arms, not his face.

"Let's go, Cody! But hang onto the railing!" No response. She pounded on him. "Move!"

He obeyed. This time when she unlatched the storm door, the wind slammed it open, shattering the window. She ignored it and pushed him into the warm house.

Karlea began trembling. "Now you can fall down. At least you won't freeze to death."

After shedding her outer clothes, she removed his rain jacket. His head, neck, and shoulders had been soaked by the snow, the rest of him by perspiration.

"Those wet clothes have to come off. Undress!" No response. "Strip! Now!"

In slow motion, he tugged at his sweatshirt without making any progress. "Raise your arms." He managed to follow that order. When she pulled it and his T-shirt over his head, he staggered. "Steady. Get your jeans off!"

While he attempted that, she hurried to retrieve a blanket and towels. She returned to find the jeans down to his knees.

"Shorts too!" He obeyed. "You're going to be so embarrassed when you can think again." She draped the blanket over his shoulders, rolled a kitchen chair to him, and braced her foot against it. "Sit!" He dropped into the chair with such force that it almost escaped.

She let her breath out, then finished removing his clothes before pushing him closer to the fireplace. She deposited several towels on the knee-high hearth and dried his hair with the same energy she had used on the filly. His neck offered little resistance, making the job harder.

"You gave me a scare, Cody." *He's been a godsend since Bill died. What would I do without him.* She shook her head. *I'd never be able to keep my horses without his help. Maybe a couple saddle horses, but not a full-fledged breeding farm. And he's even a better horse trainer than I am.*

She draped a warm, dry towel over his head, then kneeled. His blue eyes showed no hint of embarrassment. *You won't even let me see you in a swimsuit.* She rubbed the towel along his muscular thighs.

The chill left her. *What a hunk.* She pulled away, then slapped her face. *Shame on you! You used to change his diapers.* She grabbed another warm towel and draped it over his lap, wrapping his feet in a third, before tucking the blanket around him.

"Would you get embarrassed so I can quit worrying? What else can I do to warm you?" She bit her lip. "Hot chocolate."

When she returned with the beverage, he had begun shivering.

"Good boy! I know you hate it when I call you that. Tell me to quit. Shivering is good. It means the thermostat is working again. Here's fuel for the furnace. Drink!"

She held the cup while he sipped. After he finished, she finally felt comfortable leaving him. She ran upstairs to change from her wet clothes.

***

When she reentered the kitchen, he raised his head. "C-c-cold."

She let her breath out. "I know, honey. But you're a lot warmer than you were. I'll get you more hot chocolate." She offered him the mug and he reached for it. "You're shivering too much. I'll hold it." He nodded and drank. "Good boy."

"D-dang it, Karlea! Don't call me that!"

She smiled and kissed his temple. "That's better."

"You're talking weird."

"Your brain's numb. Drink."

She helped him finish, then reached under the blanket, rubbing his chest. "Hey! Quit that!"

"There's the blush I've been looking for."

"What *are* you talking about?"

"I figured you'd be out of danger when I could make you blush."

"Well, pawing me would do it."

Karlea smirked. *This is going to be fun.* "You didn't blush when you stripped for me."

"I did no such thing!"

"What are you wearing?" When he glanced under the blanket, his face turned several shades redder. "And you didn't bat an eye when I dried you."

The red crept down his neck and he barely whispered. "All of me?"

"No. Just the lower half." He looked away. "It's not like I haven't seen it before. I used to change your diapers."

"I've grown a lot since then."

"I noticed."

"You *love* tormenting me."

She stepped behind him, hugged him, and kissed his cheek. "It's nerves. You had me worried. You stopped shivering."

"Oh. No wonder I don't remember. Did I get the baby in?"

"Yes."

"The last thing I remember is coming to the corral." His brow furrowed. "Wait a minute. You *noticed?*"

Karlea's pulse quickened. "Noticed what?"

"You said you noticed my body."

She turned away, not wanting him to see her red cheeks. "It was kind of tough to ignore."

"Hm-m. Was it enough to convince you that I'm not a kid anymore?

"Wel-l. This experience will make it tougher to think of you as a kid."

"Good. Can I have some clothes?"

"Sure," she said, relieved to have an excuse to leave the room. "Sweat suit?"

"Sure."

"Good thing you keep these here for emergencies. I'll call your mom and tell her you're staying."

"She'd chew me out if I left you alone in this weather."

When Karlea called, Cody's mother answered on the first ring. "Hi, Nancy. Your baby is staying with me tonight."

Cody rolled his eyes.

"That's a relief," Nancy said. "You shouldn't be alone. They've already lost power up by Williston."

"*Wonderful.* At least it's not twenty below. The horses are in. I have plenty of dry wood. We'll be fine."

"Take care of yourselves."

"We will." Karlea disconnected. "Soup and fresh bread in about fifteen minutes."

"Good. I'm surprised you didn't tell Mom I was naked in your kitchen."

"Don't want her to think you're stormed in with a lecherous, old grandmother."

He snorted, dropping the blanket far enough to don a sweatshirt. "What are you now, granny, thirty-eight?"

"Never ask a woman her age."

"You don't even qualify for middle-age, let alone old. I guess I'll find out about the lecherous part." He laughed when she blushed. "The shoe's on the other foot."

"Never mind. Being a grandmother makes me feel old. And being a widow."

"You're not old." He struggled into sweat pants while keeping the towel in place. "You still have men drooling over you."

"Thanks. But they're probably drooling over my money. Today really made me appreciate you. I don't know what I'd have done without you the past two years."

"You would've hired someone else."

"True. But not everyone would have been so dedicated, staying overnight when a mare was due. And what you did today. That was above and beyond the call of duty. I don't tell you enough how much I appreciate you." Cody shrugged. "I know I've made you uncomfortable. But, darn it, you deserve the praise. Soup's on."

He staggered when he stood. "Whoa. I'm a little light-headed."

"Supper should help. You burned a lot of energy trying to stay warm."

"Makes sense. I'll turn in early."

"Me too, after a shower. If we lose power, that'll be a luxury for a few days."

"Good idea. I think I worked up a sweat lugging that baby."

II

Karlea opened her eyes in an unusually dark room. *No yard light. No power. The cold woke me.* Fumbling for a flashlight, she found her watch. 1:45. After locating the flashlight, she slipped on her moccasins and descended the stairs. She closed the stairway door to conserve heat, then piled kindling on the fireplace embers. The beam from Cody's flashlight appeared behind her.

"Would you close the doors into the diningroom?"

"Sure. I'll start the other fireplace too. I didn't notice we'd lost power."

Karlea pulled a chair near the fireplace and waited for him. When he sat on the hearth, she sighed. "I'm not going through another winter like this."

"I've heard that before."

"No, you haven't. I've said I don't want to."

He studied her. "You're serious."

"Yes. I have Seasonal Affective Disorder, depression brought on by long winters and lack of sunlight. The doctor wanted to put me on anti-depressants, but I convinced him to try that lamp instead."

"You said that was for your plants."

"It helps them too. When the days get longer in the spring, my depression goes away. This storm knocked my feet out from under me."

He thought a moment. "Where would you go?"

"Arizona. A week ago Dotty told me that a place I like is for sale."

"You've even looked for a place?"

"I looked *at* places when I visited. But this particular farm belongs to Hank's friends. I just liked it when I stopped there with them. I called Dotty before the storm knocked out the phones. She'll put the realtor in touch with me." She just gave him time to absorb that information.

"You've made up your mind?"

"Yes. I'd like you to go with me."

"To *Arizona!*"

"You sound like I asked you to cut off your right arm."

"Why would I go to Arizona? My family's all here. I don't know anybody there."

"You know me. And you'd keep the job you love. I'll even give you a raise. You probably won't find another horse-sitting job around here."

"I don't want to live in the desert."

"It's dry. But they live in the mountains."

"Mountains? In Arizona?"

"I know you hated Geography. But you've seen the pictures I brought back from there."

"You traveled a lot. I didn't think they were taken around Hank and Dotty's place. So it isn't all cactus?"

"The juniper trees outnumber cactus at least ten-to-one. There are other evergreens. And grass. The elevation is almost six thousand feet. It's really beautiful. The place has an indoor arena. And a swimming pool. Plenty of places to trail ride."

He stared over her shoulder. "Okay. I'll think about it."

"Thank you." She smoothed her sweatshirt. "This fire will keep the kitchen and your bedroom comfortable. Um-m, may I share your bed?"

He looked away. "I'll sleep in the chair."

"Nonsense. You need your rest. If sharing your bed is out, *I'll* sleep in the chair."

"Well ... ah-h ... well. Geez, Karlea. You're a woman. I'd be so embarrassed if ..."

She grinned. "You think you could get turned on being that close to me?"

He looked away. "Anything's possible. I've gone without a long time."

"I'm flattered. Just picture me in my stinkiest old clothes." She took his hand. "Come. We can get through this."

He shuffled after her. They climbed into bed, keeping space between them. But before long, she shivered.

He sighed. "Want to snuggle?"

"That'd be nice. Will it help if I keep my back to you?"

"Maybe." He spooned her.

"Oh, you're better than a furnace." They were quiet for a moment. "Cody, are you sniffing my hair?"

"Smells like apples. Makes me hungry."

She laughed. "Go to sleep."

She fell asleep while he savored the sensation of her body against his. *This isn't exactly how my dreams play out. But I'm in bed with Karlea. How great is that?* He sighed. *It's the best I can get as long as I can't tell her how I feel.*

Many times during the past two years, he had thought about confessing his love for her. The thought came both while awake and in his dreams. Each time the scene played out the same. Karlea listened in shocked dismay, told him she could never love him, and suggested that he find another job.

I'm not going to risk losing her friendship and my job. It's not worth it.

***

Daylight revealed low, gray clouds and wind, but the snow had stopped. Ice and snow coated every surface, six inches deep on the ground. Numerous branches, big and small, lay around the trees. No doubt some utility poles had suffered the same fate. Cody gazed out at the scene as they both dressed for chores.

"What a mess."

"Watch the steps."

"I know. You watch them too. The wind must've caught your storm door. It's sprung. We'll need to replace it."

After descending the stairs, he helped Karlea down. Then they crunched their way to the barn. He broke ice on the water tank while she turned out pregnant mares with distant foaling dates. When he herded them from the corral, the horses converged on the hay feeders.

They worked together moving young horses into one corral and near-term mares into another.

Only six mares with foals and Dan stayed inside. Cody pumped water by hand and carried pails while Karlea fed. When he walked to the stallion shed, she stayed in the barn, playing with the babies.

Later, hearing the echo of horseshoes on the concrete alley, she stepped out of a stall. "Where are you and Dan going?"

"Just the length of the driveway. I want to see if there are any power lines down in the pasture. I won't be long."

"Be careful. Don't make me come look for you again."

He grinned. She followed him outside where he mounted bareback. Dan moved off in his smooth medium gait, breaking through the ice to good footing. About 200 yards from the barn, Cody urged Dan into a lope. The gelding kicked up his heels, but Cody had no problem keeping his seat.

"That boy can ride a horse." She shook her head. "That *man* can ride a horse." She watched him disappear over a rise before returning to the babies. Twenty minutes later she heard Dan. "How does it look?"

Cody grabbed a brush before answering. "There's one pole snapped off between here and the road, but the lines aren't in the pasture. I could see two more on the main line."

"We'll be without power for a while."

"Days, not hours."

"At least I have a gas stove to cook on. How about venison sausage and eggs?"

"Sounds good. I'll dig out your camping stuff. It may come in handy before this is over."

***

That day and the next, between chores they played cards and kept the fireplaces going. While the kitchen and Cody's bedroom stayed in the sixties, temperatures in the rest of the house ranged from the fifties to near freezing.

The following day, the sky cleared and the wind switched to the south. Temperatures soared over forty degrees.

Karlea checked the phone. *Still dead.* And no signal on the cell phone. When she sat by the kitchen table with notebook and pen, Cody looked up from tending the fire.

"What now?"

"Something productive. Like deciding which horses I'll take to Arizona. I can't move all of them."

He pulled up a chair. "So you really mean it?"

"Yes."

"Okay. Do you plan to take more than you can haul in the two trailers?"

"Two trips with the nine horse and one with the three-horse."

"Will you go before the foals are weaned?"

"I have no idea. Depends how long it takes to close on a place."

"So you might not take twenty-one adult horses. List twenty-one in the order of importance. How do you plan to sell the rest?"

"I'll advertise, then look for a hunter/jumper auction for those that don't sell. Number one, Rullah. Number two, Dan."

"I haven't said I'm going."

"I'm reserving a place for Dan. If you bail on me, I'll put another horse in that spot."

"M-m. Jewel, Princess, Lena, Splash, and—I suppose—Duchess. Although I'm not feeling very charitable after she ran me over."

"That was my fault."

"You were searching for me. It's not your fault. She should have enough respect for me to avoid me under any circumstances. I'll remind her of that when the weather improves."

"Wouldn't it be great to have nice weather most days of the year?"

He grinned. "Yes, Karlea."

"And the indoor arena when it isn't nice."

"Yes, Karlea."

"And I'll finally have closer places to show my horses. My list has to include some of the youngsters you've been training."

"How many?"

"The best two."

"Kelsey and Celtic."

She nodded and wrote. "That's ten. Patches and Cat. And Lena's filly. She's fantastic."

"Yeah. Georgia?"

"Yes." She numbered the list. "That's fourteen."

"Better start culling hard. A few more babies and we're full."

"We'll sleep on it."

"Maybe in a few days. Sleeping with you, I don't think much about horses."

She blushed. "Cody, you can be such a *man*."

"I'll take that as a compliment."

"Oh, here's Ben."

She watched her older step-son alight from his pickup. He and Cody had always struck her as "real" cowboys. Tall and lean, with a long stride and eyes that constantly scanned their surroundings. When Ben entered, he hugged her and offered a gallon of milk.

"Hi, Mom. What happened to your door?"

"Wind. Thanks for the milk. We're running low. What's the news?"

"Just came from town. They have power. Saw Cody's dad. Nancy's having fits. I promised I'd check here and report back to her."

Cody shook his head. "Of course. She wouldn't be Mom if she wasn't in a tizzy about one of her kids. How bad *was* this storm?"

"The outages start north of Williston and go clear down to Bowman and Hettinger. They have line crews in from all over the country.

"How long before they get to us?" Karlea asked.

"Don't hold your breath. But check your cell phone later today. They're working near the tower. Cody's folks should get electricity soon too."

"Maybe they'll let us come over and take a shower. Want some hot chocolate? My emergency coffee leaves something to be desired."

"Sure. What's this list?"

"We're deciding which horses we're taking to Arizona."

"She's taking," Cody said.

"He hasn't decided to go yet."

Ben's brow furrowed. "This storm must've been the last straw."

"It was. Are you ready to move here?"

"Cathy will be thrilled. She's tired of the double-wide. I'll talk to my banker the next time I'm in town. Cody, I'd sure feel better if you went with Mom, at least for a while. She could get someone else to do the work, but I'd feel better having someone I trust living there with her."

"With her?"

"There are living quarters in the stable," Karlea said.

"Oh."

"Give me a year, Cody. If you hate it, you can hire someone for me and come home."

After a pause, Ben spoke. "It would be good to get out of your parents's house for a while."

Cody sighed. *Why am I torturing her? I can't let her leave without me.* "Okay. Okay."

She hugged him. "Oh, thank you, Cody."

"Yeah, thanks, Cody. You'll protect her from the gold diggers. A beautiful, young widow will be awfully tempting for some con man."

"Ben, you must think I'm really gullible."

"No. I'd hate for you to be alone in a new place. Lonely people don't always think straight."

Cody chuckled. "And you think *I'll* be thinking straight? I've never been away from home more than six weeks at a time."

"You can watch out for each other."

***

Cody insisted that he could handle evening chores, leaving Karlea free to cook a big meal. When he entered the house, he inhaled the aromas.

"Smells good in here."

"It won't be ready for at least a half-hour. I heated water in the stock pot. If you're creative, you could probably take a bath."

He grinned. "You telling me that I need one?"

"We both do. I plan to take one after supper."

"I'll run some cold water in the tub and use this to heat it up."

"Thank God for the Artesian well. We'd have to carry water from the barn without it. Oh, the cell phone works. I got a call from the realtor in Snowflake. Hank told her that I'd be without power, but she was surprised that my phones didn't work. I asked her the price and made a counter-offer."

"You're really wheeling and dealing on this."

"Don't be a wet blanket."

"Sorry. You could at least pretend to have mixed feelings about it."

"I do. I'm leaving my home of twenty years, Ben and his family, and so many friends. But, right now, I'm excited. This is the biggest adventure of my life. Try to be happy for me."

"I am." He gave her a quick hug. "I just don't like change."

"Most people don't. I think you'll like it there."

"I'm trying to keep an open mind."

"Remember, it's an adventure."

"I prefer winter camping in the Badlands."

"That's open-minded?"

III

It took the better part of two weeks for the area to recover from the ice-storm. Spring returned.

But Cody felt like nothing would ever be normal again. When he told his parents about the move, his mother began crying. For the next several days, that occurred often. But his father praised his decision.

Cody had to admit that he needed to get away from home. He was in danger of becoming one of those bachelors who live with their parents for a lifetime. *I had a normal childhood. Mom didn't start spoiling me till I was fourteen.*

When his brother, Lee, left home and she saw the empty nest looming. And it probably didn't help that I was the only kid who wasn't adopted.

"Cody." Karlea's voice penetrated his thoughts.

He pulled himself away from the window. "Huh?"

"Lunch. What has you so preoccupied?"

"Mom. She's really taking this hard."

"I feel kind of bad about that. This must be extra hard for her. I know your parents love all their kids. But having you after adopting five kids makes you pretty special. It's tough for her to let go."

"Yeah. I feel kind of bad about it too. But, even if it's tough, I need to go."

"For both of you."

He nodded and attacked his lunch. She just nibbled at her sandwich.

Now who's preoccupied? He drank, then placed his elbow on the table, chin in hand. "Tell me."

"Um-m. I'm flying down to sign the papers on the farm and take a look around next week."

"Oh." He took another bite of his sandwich.

"You should plan to move shortly after June 1st."

"Oh. That soon."

"Yeah."

"I need a firm date to give my cousins. We need to get the vet out for Coggins tests and health certificates on the first bunch. And the brand inspector."

"I'll call both this afternoon. When I'm in Taylor, I'll get a firm date. Dotty tells me the sellers are already in their new place. They're in the process of cleaning out the junk that accumulates."

"Is this place in Show Low, or Snowflake, or Taylor? You talk about all three."

"The address of the farm is Taylor. Show Low is less than twenty miles. It's a bigger city with a regional airport. So sometimes I fly in there. Snowflake is Taylor's twin town. They share a school and police department and who knows what else. You go right from one into the other."

"Oh. I guess I'll start packing when I get home tonight. Tomorrow, we should start cramming stuff into trunks and figure out how we'll fit it all into the tackrooms of the horse trailers. You've already made a good start packing up the house."

"I want you to have furniture when you get there. We'll need the moving van at least a day ahead."

"So what will I do down there till you move this fall?"

She fidgeted, then took a deep breath. "I'd like you to show Kelsey and Celtic."

"Show?"

"Hank has room for two more in his show trailer. You could just go with them."

"Show? English?"

"You ride English when you're training the horses over jumps."

"But I wear *jeans*! Not those glorified tights. I wouldn't be caught dead in those things."

"Cody! They're very comfortable. I need you to do this."

He glared at her. *I'll do anything for Karlea, but she's asking an awful lot. I should get something in return.* He reached a decision. "I want a dog."

She blinked. "A dog?"

"Yeah. I deserve something for wearing that get up."

"Of course. But I expected you to ask for a raise."

"Money isn't very good company. You've never had a dog. You'll like having one around."

"Okay. You can get a dog when you get there. I think you're letting me off easy."

"Who says I'm done making demands."

"What else do you want?"

"I haven't decided. But every time I want something, I'll remind you that you owe me big time for dressing like a pansy."

"Okay." She chuckled. "Thanks for agreeing to show. You'll be good at it."

"Yeah. If my attitude doesn't get in the way."

IV

Karlea returned from Arizona late and slept in the next morning. While pouring her first cup of coffee, she saw Cody's pickup parked by the barn. When she finished the cup, she filled two travel mugs and joined him in the tack room.

"Coffee?"

He quit trying to stuff saddle pads into a trunk. "Sure. What's the word?"

"Do you want the good news or the bad news first?"

"Bad."

"The apartment in the stable is horrendous. I'd only seen the ground floor, which isn't bad. The bedroom upstairs has light showing through the walls in a couple places. It's so poorly insulated, you'd have to sleep downstairs on a couch in the winter. And probably during the heat of the summer too."

"I thought they had a trainer living there."

"It turns out they hired someone in the spring, not telling the person about the apartment. As soon as it got cold, he'd quit."

"So where will I live? I don't want to look for a place when I get there."

"And I need you on the farm. The house has four bedrooms and three-and-a-half baths. Would you mind living there with me?"

He added another saddle pad to the trunk to hide just how much he liked that idea. His chest felt tight at the thought of spending even more time with her.

"Well. Part of the attraction of moving was to finally live on my own. But I guess if you don't act like Mom, it would work."

"I promise. I won't. Your room will be your space. If you want to live like a slob, just keep the door closed. You'll do your own laundry. I'll just cook for us."

"That sounds okay. Guess I'll have to learn to do laundry. I even brought it home from horseshoing school. I can cook. But I don't mind if you do. I don't think I'll be a slob."

"You'll have to cook till I get there."

"How long?"

"I suppose I need to wait till after the foals are weaned."

"September?" She nodded. "I'd better get that dog as soon as I get there."

"You'll have your cousins for a couple weeks. And I'm sure Hank, Dotty, and Kate will make you feel welcome."

"Who's Kate?"

"Hank's daughter. She's about your age. She shows their horses, so you'll be spending quite a bit of time with her. When do you plan to leave?"

"Jeff and Art finish classes on the tenth. They want at least a week to relax before they go to work. If we put a real push on, we should be able to get the stuff done here so we can leave by the second. I'm glad they'll be helping you this summer. There'll still be a lot of work to do."

"I know. I've scheduled the auction for August 14th to get it done before they go back to school."

Nancy's voice interrupted their conversation. "Hello!"

"Down here, Mom!" Cody called.

She joined them in the tackroom. "I just stopped to visit."

"Hope you don't mind visiting while we pack," Karlea said. "We have to get busy."

"Not at all."

When her eyes began to tear, Cody threw up his hands. "Mom, put this in perspective! You have friends with kids overseas where people are shooting at them. I'm going to *Arizona!*" He stalked out while she wiped her eyes.

Karlea rubbed her arm. "I know it's tough when your baby leaves home. I've been there. But he's right."

"I know. Allen has scolded me too. He says I'm part of the reason Cody wants to leave."

"He doesn't *want to* leave. I had to twist his arm. But, Nancy, he knows that he needs to. Maybe he'll start dating again. I'll try not to work him so hard that he doesn't have a social life."

"I've worried about that too. It must be more than three years since he's dated. I don't think I'm to blame for that. I never criticized his girlfriends."

"I don't think you're to blame either. When I asked him about it, he just said they're too much bother."

They heard his footsteps before he entered and resumed his work without a word.

Nancy took a deep breath. "I'm sorry, Cody. You're right. Will you come home for Christmas?"

"Sure. If this woman isn't too much of a slave driver."

"Ha! You drive yourself harder than I do. You can come home. I'll invite my kids, so I won't be alone."

V

Jeff and Art brought horses from the barn while Cody and Karlea loaded them into the nine horse trailer. First three mares with foals, then two yearlings and the show mare. Cody put the stallion, Rullah, in the three horse trailer, Dan, and finally, the show gelding.

He latched the gate and waved his cousins to their vehicles. He hugged his mother and wiped tears from her cheeks. "I'll be fine."

"I know."

Then Karlea hugged him. "Be careful. Call me every night or if you have trouble."

"Sure. Don't worry. Everything's in good working order. All the tires are new. We have tools. We're prepared."

"You always have everything under control. You're *so* special. Thank you."

He kissed her forehead. "Yeah."

He climbed into the pickup and pulled out of the yard with the nine-horse trailer. The other pickup and moving van followed. When he glanced in the mirror he saw his mother and Karlea with their arms around each other.

He let his breath out and spoke to the empty cab. "I sure hope I'm doing the right thing."

***

"We made it. All the horses are settled in. They ran around for a while, but now most of them are laying down."

"That's a relief," Karlea said. "I thought you'd call sooner. Any problems?"

"Yeah. The transmission on the blue pickup started acting up after we turned south off I-40. I think we're losing overdrive. Dotty's made a list of the best places to go for things I'll need. It includes a trustworthy mechanic. I'll call tomorrow. If it can't be fixed by the time Jeff and Art head back, I'll have them take the silver one."

"Let me know when he gives you a cost estimate. If it's too much, we'll trade for a new one. It's getting up there in miles."

"Okay."

"Did you have help unloading?"

"Hank and Kate were waiting when we got here. They had everything ready. Dotty showed up before we finished with a great picnic supper. It's hot and windy here, but it's not unbearable. Not humid like it can get at home. She brought juice and muffins for breakfast tomorrow. When they left, we went for a swim."

"I don't suppose you unloaded much furniture."

"Mattresses. That's why I made sure they were next to the door. We wanted something comfortable to sleep on. We'll finish unloading in the morning, before it gets too hot."

"Sounds like you have things under control."

"Hope so. I'll call tomorrow evening."

"Okay. You know, I miss you already."

Cody grinned, relieved that she could not see it. *Maybe moving wasn't such a bad idea.* "I left you with a lot more work to do."

"You took most of the high maintenance horses with you. Everything here is on pasture."

"So you really *do* miss me."

"That's what I said."

"Well, I'll probably miss you too when things settle down around here."

"I like the sound of that. If you like having me around, you won't run back to North Dakota."

"Unless I get too homesick before you get here."

***

Cody sat back in the recliner and sighed, a glass of ice water in his hand. His cousins had headed north a few hours earlier. He enjoyed the quiet. Jeff and Art still acted too much like teenagers—loud music and loud behavior. They called him a wet blanket.

They're right. When did I start acting like an adult? He thought about that a moment. *After Bill died. Karlea really needed me and I decided it was time to grow up.*

She depends on me. Now, if I can just get her to fall in love with me. It sure won't hurt living in the same house. The thought of brushing against her in the hallway sent stimulating sensations throughout his body. *Get your mind out of the gutter. You don't want to seduce her, you want her to fall in love with you.*

He pulled his mind back to the quiet house. *I wonder if I will get homesick. I like this.*

Molly, the Golden Retriever, thumped her tail on the floor. She lay on her side, her belly shaved because the animal rescue place had insisted that she be spayed before he took her home. Just under a year old, she had taken an instant liking to him.

He had already developed his new routine. He woke just before dawn and did chores at sunrise, enjoying the cool, mountain air. After breakfast, he rode the two hunters, worked with foals, checked the irrigation, and finished as many outdoor chores as he could before the wind started blowing. He took an hour at lunchtime to relax before cleaning the few stalls in use, then working in the house, shop, or tackroom.

The phone interrupted his relaxation. He picked it up without leaving the chair. "Dakota del Norte."

"I like the sound of that. You had a good idea."

"Hi, Karlea. I'm a genius. And you're calling during my siesta."

"It's the best time. You're tough to reach in the evening."

"I could say I'm working hard. Sometimes I'm treating the pool. But more likely I'm in the pool. Or riding Dan."

"Do you know how to treat a pool?"

"Dotty showed me. Hank taught me about irrigation. It took quite a while. The pastures and hay field are flood irrigated. The trees and garden have a drip system on timers. You just have to make sure none of the nozzles are plugged. I talked to one of the Navaho County master gardeners to find out how to take care of the vegetables the sellers planted."

"What kind?"

"Tomatoes, cucumbers, lettuce, and a bunch of peppers. You really have to keep them watered. Between the heat and the wind, they wilt in a hurry. Did you know that the trees in the back yard are apples, pears, plums, and apricots?"

"They told me. Are you lonely yet?"

"No. I like the quiet. I tried to work Jeff and Art hard enough so they'd go to sleep at night."

"Did it work?"

"Partly. They kept calling me a slave driver and a wet blanket. I told them they weren't here on vacation."

"If you drive everyone else like you drive yourself, you're a tough boss. Did you give them any time for sightseeing?"

"Sure. We took Sunday off. We drove down to the Salt River Canyon."

"Oh, that's a pretty drive. Did they enjoy it?"

"Yeah. So did I. Not something you see at home. We stopped in Show Low on the way back, had supper, and took in a movie."

"Good. How's your dog?"

"Mellow, so far. But she could still be recovering from her surgery."

"What do you have on your schedule?"

"I have an appointment to talk to the Vo Ag teacher later today. He should be able to help me find a couple kids to work this summer."

"Just don't be a slave driver with them."

Cody chuckled. "Okay. Kate is taking me to Flagstaff to buy those goofy show clothes tomorrow afternoon. You can't even buy those things around here. My kind of place."

"Cody! You got your dog. Now quit complaining."

"I said I'd wear the clothes. I didn't say I'd quit complaining."

"You'll give me gray hair. Talk to you tomorrow."

***

Kate Carlson, a year older than Cody with short, auburn hair and a muscular build, had been riding horses since before she could walk. And for most of her life, she had been riding jumping horses. She taught him show etiquette, correcting him when he rode the show hunters like a cowboy.

Now, she helped him select show clothes. "Cody, would you come out of that dressing room?"

"Oh, all right."

He skulked through the curtain wearing a short-sleeved shirt and tie with form-fitting breeches that ended just above his ankle. He scowled, but she smiled, circling him.

"Very nice."

"I look like a pansy."

She edged within a foot of him. "Hardly. It's very sexy."

He blushed, but grinned. "I'll bet you say that to all the guys in breeches."

"Only the ones with the body for it. I've been looking forward to this."

His grin broadened. "Kate, are you coming on to me?"

"I'm expressing interest."

He studied her, surprised that he, too, felt interested. He scolded himself. *That's because you're not thinking with your brain.* He leaned down and kissed her cheek.

"Let's work on friendship before we go there. I prefer to move slowly with these things."

She smiled. "That's refreshing. Is this typical of North Dakota men?"

"Doubt it. I never was much for one-night stands."

"You're making a good impression. Do you have anything against going out to dinner with a friend?"

"Well, we already had lunch together. But it's better than eating alone."

"Tomorrow evening?"

"Sure."

"I'll pick you up."

"Why?"

"It's on my way to town. Six too early?"

"No. Can I change out of these clothes now? Informal dinner?"

"Yes to both. But you need a jacket for showing."

"They look like suit jackets." He returned to the dressing room. "Couldn't I just get one at a second hand store? There's one on every other block in this state."

"Maybe. Not just any suit jacket would work. But you might find something."

"I can't see spending all that money on something I won't use much."

"It's not your money."

"I'm as tight with Karlea's money as I am with mine."

"Hope she appreciates that. When will you and your horses be ready to show?"

"I'll never be ready. The horses seem to have adjusted to the altitude. I guess they're ready."

"Plan on going with us the weekend after next."

"I hope I can have a couple kids working by then. I'm interviewing this weekend."

"Dotty will check on your horses while you're gone. Just to make sure your help is dependable."

"Dotty's great. She must be your step-mom?"

"Dotty? She's my aunt, Dad's sister."

"Oh. So your dad's single?"

"Yeah. When I was eight, my mom decided she didn't want to be tied down anymore. Dad and Dotty moved here two years later. Montana doesn't have any longer riding season than North Dakota does."

"Oh."

She laughed. "Why do you think Dad was so anxious to have Karlea move down here? He's had the hots for her for years."

Cody clenched his fists, surprised by the wave of jealousy he felt, relieved that Kate could not see it. He pulled his T-shirt on. "Really? Is the feeling mutual?"

"Not! She thinks of him as a big brother. Seeing him more often won't change that."

He let his breath out. The competition held no advantage. "I suppose we should hit some second-hand stores to find the rest of my costume."

"You can be such a *cowboy*."

"I'll take that as a compliment."

VI

Cody stroked Kelsey's neck while they waited for their turn in the arena. Earlier, the gelding had placed sixth in a halter class of eight. Celtic had fared better in her class, third of ten. But halter classes were beauty contests and Celtic looked prettier than her stablemate. They would face each other in this novice hunter class and be judged on their ability.

"Now entering the ring, from Dakota del Norte Stable, Dakota Kelsey, ridden by Cody Pfeiffer."

Cody gathered the reins and Kelsey came alert. He rode in at a trot, then switched to a canter, maintaining the even hunter speed required by the class. Kelsey took the small jumps without knocking down any rails, a clean round.

When they left the arena, he rode to Hank and Celtic, dismounted, loosened Kelsey's girth, then did the opposite with Celtic.

"Good round, Cody. Now one more just like it."

Cody nodded and led Celtic a short distance before mounting. He rode in large circles until the announcer called them.

"Next up, from Dakota del Norte, Dakota Celtic, ridden by Cody Pfeiffer."

He felt Celtic's tension. When he asked for a canter, she gave him a gallop instead. He tried to ease her speed, but approached the first jump too fast. She buried herself too close, but despite the awkward take-off that caused, she cleared it. When she landed, he kept working to slow her, but she buried herself on the second approach also. Again, an ungraceful jump. She finally accepted his guidance upon touching down.

She finished the course looking like a hunter. Cody left the arena shaking his head.

Hank grinned. "We know danged well that was her nerves, not yours. She'll get better with experience."

"Their performance at home doesn't really mean anything when you get to a show."

"That's right. You're a heck of a rider. I've seen plenty dumped when their horses decided to jump like a goat."

Cody dismounted, chuckling, and patted her neck. "This was just new and scary for you, wasn't it, girl. You'll get used to it. Between this huge arena and the crowd, this is nothing like home."

"Karlea has an eye for horses. She kept a couple of good ones."

Cody felt no need to tell Hank that Karlea had consulted him before keeping these two horses. They always made those decisions together. Hank saw him as just a hired man. Karlea depended on him for so much more.

***

"... so Kelsey placed second and Celtic didn't place," Cody said into the phone.

Karlea chuckled. "Big surprise. When's your next show?"

"Two weeks. Up in Utah. We'll be staying overnight in Hank's camper. That should be interesting."

"Kate might want to sleep with you."

"Right! With her dad there."

"Hank's a very liberal dad."

"No one's that liberal. I told her I like to move slow."

"Have you two been on any more dates?"

"It wasn't a date."

"Sure, it wasn't."

"Karlea! It was Dutch. Supper with a friend. I *am* lonely here without you."

"Okay. Okay. I can't wait to get down there. Why didn't I move and have you come in September?"

"You were afraid I'd back out."

"True. By the way, you didn't answer my question. Are you and Kate going out again?"

"Tomorrow evening. Better than eating alone."

"How are the new employees working out?"

"So far, so good. They'll both be juniors next year, so hopefully we'll have them for a couple years. They're both in 4-H horse clubs. They've done a lot of riding *and* they know how to care for horses. Kevin does his work and he's ready to leave. But Jill would hang around for hours if she could."

"Just be careful. You don't want to spend time alone with a teenaged girl."

"I know. I visited both sets of parents before they started. I invited them to drop by unannounced anytime. I told Jill's parents, if Kevin can't work, I'll call them. They can choose not to have her work alone with me."

"Sounds like you've taken precautions. Do you work shirtless around her?"

He laughed. "I put my shirt on for their interviews, but didn't snap it. I didn't hire the girls who drooled. So, yes, I work shirtless around Jill. She's still more interested in horses than guys."

When Karlea stopped laughing, she offered a word of caution. "Just remember, my first crush was on a horse trainer. When a horse-crazy girl finally notices boys, it's usually cowboys. You're sexy enough to activate a dormant female libido."

"I haven't activated yours."

She just sputtered for a while. Then she had a comeback. "Are you sure?"

Since she could not see him blush, he tried to sound suave. "Why, Karlea, you've been keeping secrets from me. We'll have to discuss this when you get here."

"Don't get any ideas. I don't act on every thought that crosses my mind. When I start to notice how sexy you are, I remind myself that I used to change your diapers."

"Great! Reality is what you see, not what you remember."

"I know you hate it when I remind you of that. But seriously, you should talk down to Jill. Talk down to both of them. You don't want to appear biased. It will make you less appealing."

"I can't do that. You didn't do that to me. I don't want to turn into Bill."

"You're right. I used to hate how he treated the hired help. I just don't want you to find yourself backed into a stall one day."

"I promise to be careful. I'd better go to bed. It's been a long day."

"Good night, Cody."

"Night."

He held the phone after he disconnected, thoughts of her racing through his mind. He remembered the warmth of her body in his arms, the scent of her hair, and the way her T-shirt would cling when she perspired. His body ached.

"How can you miss what you've never had?" Molly thumped her tail on the floor and came to him. He stroked her head. "Good girl. Yeah. I'm talking to myself again." He smiled. "But she's noticed my body. In a good way. That'll make it easier to get her to fall in love with me."

***

Kate showed up for their next non-date wearing low-rider stretch jeans and a halter top. Cody drove into Show Low, noticing that he liked the scent of her perfume.

She gave him directions to the Porter Mountain Steakhouse. "I have reservations."

A hostess led them to a corner table with candles and low light. Cody glanced around.

"This looks more like a setting for a romantic date."

Kate rubbed her foot up his leg. "Let's go with that."

"What part of slow don't you understand?"

"Do you consider me a friend?"

"Sure."

"You said that you wanted to become friends first. Mission accomplished. Let's become friends with benefits. No strings attached."

He studied her over his menu, for the first time noticing that she wore nothing under her halter top. A heart-shaped garnet necklace invited his eyes to her nice cleavage. He raised his menu to block the view.

"Sounds like I'm being invited to a one-night stand."

She chuckled. "If you're any good, I'll give you as many nights as you want. Afternoons too. You can't hide forever."

Cody stared at the menu without seeing it, very aware of his rapid pulse. *It's been so long. But it would be wrong. And I'd be cheating on Karlea.* He glanced at Kate. *But it's been so long.*

The waitress came to take their drink orders, giving him a reprieve from his thoughts. He chose iced tea.

"No alcohol tonight. I'm driving." *That's not the only reason I need good judgement.*

When the waitress departed, Kate ran her foot up his leg again. She licked her lips. "Your eyes tell me you want it."

He glared. "And if you don't get too pushy, you might get it."

She turned serious. "Is that what turns you on? You want me to be coy?"

"You can't be what you're not. But if you keep pushing me, I'll take a cold shower rather than give you what you want."

"Okay. I guess I've noticed this stubborn streak. Consider this an open invitation. Whenever you want it, let me know."

"Thank you. Your other approach was going to destroy our friendship."

"Sorry. I haven't had much experience with this sort of thing. I usually have to tell guys no sex on the first date."

"But the second one is fine?"

"Depends. If it's somebody like you—a friend, yes. If I don't know him very well, then it takes about four dates to get me in bed. That gives me time to figure out if I even like him. Or if we'll have anything to talk about when we're not otherwise occupied. What do you look for in a woman?"

"That's a good question. I'll have to think about it. I haven't looked in a long time. I don't have time to date."

The waitress brought drinks and took their order. When she left, Kate resumed the conversation.

"What do you mean, no time to date?"

"Since Bill died, Karlea's really needed me. My last girlfriend got jealous. When she told me I had to choose, it wasn't hard. I knew that I didn't love her. But I really love my job."

"So you haven't been on a date since Bill died?"

"Not quite that long. Almost three years."

"And you're not into one-night stands." She raised her eyebrows. "So no sex during that time either?"

He smiled and shook his head. "And, believe me, that's not always easy. But it's not impossible. Despite what some men think."

"Does Karlea realize what you've given up for her?"

He blushed. "I don't think of it like that. And I know she appreciates me. That means a lot."

"She'd better. Not many men are that dedicated to their work."

VII

When Cody opened the door for their next non-date, Kate stood outside holding a paper sack and a pizza box.

"I thought we were going out."

"I brought pizza, beer, and a movie instead. Are you disappointed?"

"Depends. What kind of movie and pizza?"

"Action. Half supreme and half Italian sausage."

"You done good."

He took the pizza box, for the first time noticing her outfit. A pale pink, sleeveless blouse with enough of the top buttons unfastened to expose the pink bra underneath, and a denim miniskirt barely long enough to cover the essentials.

She extracted a DVD and held it up for his approval. It took him a moment to focus on it. He nodded.

She smiled. "Do you like light beer too?"

He shrugged. "It's all the same to me. I don't drink much. But I like it with pizza."

"I'm three for three. This is my lucky night."

They locked eyes for several seconds.

"Looks like you're trying to get lucky. I said no pushing."

"This is me *not* pushing. This is me issuing an engraved invitation. I thought you might loosen up on your own turf."

He scowled. "I'll get paper plates and napkins. Make yourself at home."

When he returned from the kitchen, he stared at her on the sofa, nicely tanned legs extended. He felt overdressed.

She smiled. "Want to slip into something more comfortable? Take off whatever you like. I won't mind."

Can she read my mind? "This isn't pushing?"

"It's inviting."

"Ah-h. I see. Be right back."

Cody retreated to his room, struggling to control his body. *Why am I even thinking about this? I've been faithful to Karlea for three years. Why now?* He removed his shirt. *How can she trust me if I start screwing around as soon as we're apart?*

He reminded himself that Karlea had no interest in him. He changed from jeans to cutoffs and pulled on a T-shirt.

When Kate saw him, she stuck out her lower lip. "I see more than that whenever I'm here. You never wear a shirt."

"Sure I do."

"Take it off."

"No."

"Please. Ple-ease."

He studied her a moment longer. *I want to take everything off.* He dispatched the shirt.

"That's better. She patted the sofa beside her. "I put the rest of the beer in the fridge. Can't stand warm beer."

Cody opened a bottle and downed nearly half before he joined her. They ate and watched the movie in silence. He finished his beer and took another bite. Pizza sauce dripped on his chest. Before he could wipe it off, she caught his hand.

"Let me get that for you."

He did not resist, could not even manage a protest. When he felt her tongue on his chest, he gasped as if someone had stabbed him. She resumed eating with her eyes on the TV, but a satisfied smile on her face.

His shudder turned into trembling. He had to remind himself to breath. He bolted to the kitchen to give himself time.

When he stopped shaking and his heart stopped pounding, he opened another beer. *Why am I drinking? I need to think straight.* He drank. *I don't want to think straight.*

He returned to the livingroom door and watched her while he finished the beer. She just smiled. He placed the empty bottle around the corner on the kitchen counter.

"I don't have protection."

"I do."

"Thought you would. Did I mention it's been three years?"

"Yes. How do you feel about encores?"

"Encores are usually the best part of my performance."

"I like the sound of that."

"Take your blouse off."

She complied, grinning. "I've really been looking forward to this."

"Well, duh." He took his time reaching her.

She kneeled on the sofa. While she finished undressing him, he unhooked her bra. Then he pulled her to her feet. The kiss that followed lasted long enough for him to find the zipper in the back of her skirt and remove the garment. She had seen no need for underwear.

He lowered both of them to the sofa.

***

Cody knew that his throbbing head would explode if he opened his eyes. *How long can I lay here before I have to do chores?* That would depend on the time, which he did not want to open his eyes to check.

The phone rang.

"Oh, God!" He reached for it, but someone blocked his path. *Kate!* He sat up. "Don't ...!"

Too late. She answered the phone. "Hello."

"Oh, I must have the wrong number." The voice on the other end of the line said.

"Karlea?"

"Kate?"

"Yeah. Surprise!"

Cody could only sit with his head in his hands.

"I'll say! Did you have a sleep over last night?"

"Well, we didn't get much sleep. We had a great time. But now he's acting hung over and he only had two beers."

"That's about all it takes for him. He can't hold his liquor. After two, you can get him to do about anything."

"Why, Karlea, you sound like the voice of experience."

"Kate! Not that! We celebrated after haying last year. I talked him into doing something silly. Then I talked him into doing something even sillier. So I started wondering just how impaired he was. I convinced him to let me paint his toenails. Boy, was he mad the next morning."

Kate laughed. "That's a good one. But you should've taken him to bed. You would've had a lot more fun and he wouldn't have been mad."

He had heard enough. "Give me the phone!"

"Is he always this grouchy in the morning?"

"Only when he's hung over."

"I'll let you talk to him while I make coffee."

She handed the phone to Cody, who said nothing.

"Feel pretty tough?"

"My own fault. I know my limitations. I was just stupid last night."

"You needed to unwind. Don't be so hard on yourself. I need to talk to you this morning, but I can call back in an hour."

"Thanks."

"Okay. Bye."

He took the maximum safe dose of pain reliever, then hit the shower before he joined Kate in the kitchen. She had not bothered to dress.

"Do you think you should put some clothes on?"

She placed coffee in front of him. "Why? Are you expecting company?"

"No."

"Then, no. I'm comfortable. Want a bagel?"

"Sure. Thanks."

He had just finished his second cup of coffee when the phone rang. He had brought it to the table with him. "Hello, Karlea."

"You sound a little better."

"Head feels a little better. Mouth doesn't taste so bad. And I've had a shower.

"Is Kate still with you?"

"Oh, yeah. She's all here."

"We'll talk about that later. A guy made me an offer on the rest of the mare/foal pairs. I'm just not sure if I should take it."

"How much?"

"$17,500."

"For five pair. You're asking twenty, so that's giving him the cheapest mare. When will he take them?"

"This week."

"He'll haul them?"

"Yes."

"He's not asking for any special favors?"

"Just the price."

"Have him meet you at the bank with the cash or a money order, something that won't bounce. Get it deposited and help him load horses. This will save you a lot of headaches."

"That's what I thought. But I was afraid I was giving up too much."

"Saves you taking them to an auction. You knew the answer. You just needed to bounce it off me."

"Thanks. I do that a lot. Will you be home this evening?"

"Sure. I'll be wiped out the rest of the day."

"I'll call then."

"Okay."

Cody disconnected and drank coffee, which Kate had replenished.

She smiled at him. "Karlea says you'll do anything after a couple beers."

"Not anything.   But I have impaired judgement and very little conscience."

"You wouldn't have slept with me without alcohol?"

"I didn't say that. I wanted what you had to offer, so I drank. It was the only way to shut up my conscience."

"You're feeling *guilty*?"

"Yeah."

"Why?"

"I promised myself I'd wait till I can be with the woman I love. My word isn't worth much."

"So there's someone back in North Dakota?"

"Yes."

"What she doesn't know won't hurt her."

"I can't live like that."

"You don't want to do this again?"

"No."

"I think you really mean it this time."

He sighed. "Thanks for last night. I think I needed to get it out of my system. To remind myself that it's not what I really want. I'm sorry that I used you."

"Hey, I had fun and I don't feel guilty. The encore out by the pool was especially fun. Call me if you change your mind. But if that's out, I can handle friendship."

"Thanks, Kate. I need a friend more than a lover."

***

"How do you feel tonight?" Karlea asked.

Cody sighed. "Just tired."

"Now, about your sleep over ..."

"I'm sorry. It won't happen again."

"What? Where did that come from? You don't owe me an apology. I was just teasing you. You're an adult. I can't treat you like a child just because you live under my roof."

"It still won't happen again. I feel guilty. Felt guilty even before I did it."

"So you drank."

"Yeah."

"That's what I figured. You hate hangovers. Whatever decision you make, do what's right for you. Don't put me into the equation. I want you to feel like that's your home too. If you have an overnight guest, she'll be welcome as long as you can still go to work the next morning."

"I'll keep that in mind."

"Good. We needed to clear the air about that before you worried too much."

"I *was* afraid you'd be mad."

"I want you to be happy, Cody. You won't stick around if you aren't."

"I want that for you too."

"I know. Get a good night's sleep. I'll call tomorrow."

Cody disconnected and shook his head. *Not put her into the equation?*

I never make a decision without putting her into the equation. "She would know that if I ever told her."

VIII

Cody placed Kelsey's foot on the ground and straightened from his shoeing posture. He smiled at Jill. "Done. You can put him back in his stall."

While she did that, he stowed his horseshoing tools and removed his farrier's apron. She returned as he reached for a towel.

He wiped his face, not noticing her eyes travel from his bare chest down to his jeans. She handed him his water bottle

"Thanks, and thanks for staying late to hold him. I can shoe horses in the cross ties. But they just seem to like it better when someone talks to them."

"No problem. I want to learn all I can. I'm still considering horseshoing as a career."

"It's a lot of work. I could show you how to trim feet and let you practice. That way you can figure out if you want to work that hard."

"That would be great. Thanks. You've taught us so much already. Working here is sure better than working at Sonic or McDonald's."

"But you get to see all your friends working there."

"All my real friends are horse people. I see most of them at 4-H."

"That's kind of the story of my life too."

She followed him toward the barn door, but stopped at Dan's stall. "What breed is Dan?"

Cody chuckled. "His mother came from Karlea's herd, so he's a quarter Thoroughbred. I leased her from Karlea to raise a foal of my own. She about fainted when I told her I didn't plan to breed the mare to Rullah. I wanted a smooth horse for chores. Dan's sire is a Tennessee Walker."

Jill laughed. "Did she try to talk you out of it?"

"No. She asked me to explain. When she heard my reasons, she accepted my decision."

"You really like her don't you."

Cody tensed. "You think I would've moved to Arizona if she was a rotten boss?"

"I suppose not. When do we get to meet her?"

"Don't know if she's planning to come before she moves. If she doesn't, it'll be September. You should probably get going. I don't want your parents to worry."

"I have all kinds of time. They won't be home till late."

Her eyes said more than her words. Cody wanted to rush for the door, but managed to keep his pace relaxed.

"I'm getting company tonight. I have to get ready."

"Okay. I'll see you tomorrow."

"Sure." He strode to the house while she climbed into her car. He closed the door and leaned against it. "Karlea, why'd you have to be right?"

***

Kate mounted her horse just before sunrise. "July isn't the time to be riding the washes. People ride there during the winter."

"You didn't have to come along." Cody swung up on Dan. "You told me that once the monsoons start, it won't be safe for a long time."

"Yeah. There can be quicksand."

"And, even though it's getting close to monsoon season, they don't come till the afternoon."

"You're learning."

Without dismounting, he opened the gate leaving the farm, then closed it after she rode through. "So, it's safe to ride this morning. It's only a mile from here."

"But it can get really hot down there during the summer."

"We'll only ride a couple hours. If it's as deep as you say, we should be in the shade most of the time. And, again, I didn't ask you to come along."

"There's no way I was going to let a northerner do this alone."

"Well, he's not changing his mind, so quit trying."

They followed the paved road to the edge of Karlea's property, then took a little-used dirt road that bordered the farm. Both Kate and Hank had referred to these "roads" as "goat paths." Cody had driven it to check the fence line and found spots that challenged his four-wheel-drive pickup.

On a level stretch, they loped their horses. But as they neared the wash, the road deteriorated further. The monsoons had cut through the road, leaving gullies from a foot to six feet deep. Cattle and all-terrain vehicles had made trails across the depressions.

Shaggy bark juniper trees became more plentiful near the wash. Cody could see cottonwood trees towering above its rim.

When they entered a gully with a sandy bottom, Kate stayed there, following it to the wash.

"It's like a beach here," Cody said. "I wondered how there could be quicksand."

"Drift sand from our wonderful winds. But some places have exposed bedrock too. You can't take this all the way to our place because you run into a rock wall. It's a pretty impressive waterfall during monsoons."

They rode in silence while Cody tried to get the nerve to tell her about Jill. She helped him.

"You have something on your mind. Spill it."

He did, telling her everything except Karlea's warning.

First, Kate grinned. Then, she began laughing. She finally had to stop her horse to keep herself in the saddle.

He glared. "It's not funny."

"Yes, it is. Jill has a crush on you. Face it, Cody. Women want you."

"I told you because I need your help. I didn't intend to entertain you."

"Tell her about your girlfriend in North Dakota."

"Well. That might work."

"Or, here's an idea." She nudged her horse forward. "When I come, we could do some tongue wrestling. She'd be able to see that you're taken."

"Well. Maybe. No-o. Probably not."

"Are you afraid you'll want a little more Kate?"

"No." He sighed. "Maybe."

She shook her finger at him. "Shame on you. I'm telling your girlfriend."

"First you'd have to find out who she is."

"You'd tell me if I got you drunk again."

"That ain't going to happen."

"You're no fun with a hangover anyhow. If you don't like my solutions, ask Karlea."

"I can't. She told me if I talked down to Jill, this wouldn't happen. I couldn't do it."

"That probably would've worked."

"I know. I know. But I would have felt like a jerk. Do you suppose I could just tell Jill that I'm not interested? Or explain to her that I could end up in jail if I got involved with her?"

"Don't use the last one. She'll just bat her eyes and say, 'I'll never tell.' You need to let her know that you're not interested. But, if you come right out and say it, she might feel humiliated."

Cody guided Dan through a section of boulder-strewn bedrock. "You're not helping as much as I hoped you would."

"You just don't like my suggestions. The only one you haven't axed is talking about your girlfriend. By the way, if you're so infatuated, why don't you talk about her? And why don't you have her picture somewhere?"

"How do you know I don't?"

"I've looked."

Cody shot her a scowl. "You've been snooping?"

"Yeah."

"Well, stop it. How I show my love is none of your business."

"If you showed it the way you showed me, she wouldn't be back in North Dakota."

"Just drop it."

"Okay. I know when I've struck a nerve. We'll go back to Jill. I don't have any other ideas. We wouldn't have to tongue wrestle. Just a little kiss when I come and another when I leave. She should get the picture."

He rode in silence for a moment, then stopped under the shade of a cottonwood tree. "I'll give it a try. When can you come over again?"

"Not tomorrow. Thursday."

"I'll try to keep her at bay till then."

***

The next day, like every day since he had become aware of the problem, Cody planned the work schedule to keep Jill and Kevin together at all times. The plan evaporated just after they arrived.

"I'm sorry, Cody," Kevin said. "I chipped a tooth. Mom got me a dentist appointment at one today. I hope you can get along without me."

"Sure." Cody cringed inside. "You have to take care of yourself. You two get to work. I have some calls to make."

He could have called from the tackroom, but retreated to the house. He tried Kate's cell phone.

"What's up, lover?"

"Not funny. Kevin has to leave at noon. Are you sure you can't come over?"

"No can do. Dad and I are going to look at a horse. We won't be back till this evening. Can you send her home?"

"Not without making her suspicious. I can't be alone with her. I'm sure she's about to make her move."

"Call Dotty. Have her drop by for a visit. I know she's working this morning and can't answer her phone, but leave a message."

"But what would I tell her?"

"Your underage employee has the hots for you and you're scared to death."

"I can't tell her that."

"If you tell Dotty the truth, she'll help out. If not, she won't have any reason to come over. Which would you rather be, embarrassed a little, or arrested as a pedophile?"

"I see your point. Thanks."

He disconnected and punched Dotty's number. After four rings, he heard her voice.

"Hi, this is Dotty. You know what to do when this thing beeps."

Cody covered his eyes and waited for the beep. "Dotty, this is Cody. I need a favor. Are you free this afternoon? If you could come over about noon or so, I'd really appreciate it. I'll explain when you get here." He placed the phone in the cradle and gazed at the barn. "I need a plan B."

    ***

For the first time in days, Cody kept his shirt on, no matter how much he perspired. When Kevin left for his appointment with no sign of Dotty, Cody put plan B into effect.

"Jill, why don't you bring Lena from the corral."

"Okay. Just let Snowflake follow along?"

"Sure. She'll be fine."

By the time Jill returned with the mare and filly, he had retrieved a saddle and bridle from the tackroom.

"You're going to ride her?"

"No. You're going to ride her."

Jill grinned. "Great! But why?"

"You said you wanted to try jumping. And your horse isn't going to make a jumper. I can't let you ride the show horses. Lena could use the exercise. She's sensible and she's not too old to go back to work."

"Will I get to jump today?"

"No. She's lost her girlish figure. She needs a lot of conditioning before she takes any fences. You'll need to ride her every day you're here."

"Thanks. This means so much to me. Are you going to let Kevin ride too?"

"Yeah. But he doesn't want to go near an English saddle. I'll probably have him ride some of the other mares and pony their foals. I haven't had time to do that myself. Saddle her, grab a helmet, and meet me in the arena."

He walked to the arena, confident that he could keep Jill busy for at least an hour. He prayed that Dotty would arrive before then.

***

Cody explained several stretching exercises and watched Jill work Lena through them. He had her ride the mare at a walk and trot over poles laid on the ground. She rode circles, figure eights, serpentines. He continued until he noticed Lena's ears pinned back, her patience wearing thin.

And still no sign of Dotty.

"Okay. You can groom her and give her a bath. But don't put her away. I'll be back in a few minutes."

He called Dotty from the tackroom, getting voice mail again. Not bothering to leave a message, he chewed his lip. He would have to move on to plan C and hope Dotty came. He had no plan D.

When he reached the wash rack, Jill had begun spraying Lena while

Snowflake avoided the water. Cody retrieved a foal halter.

"This is as good a time as any to teach Snowflake about baths." He turned in time to catch a stream of water in the chest. "Hey!"

Jill giggled. "Gotcha."

"Are you trying to get fired?"

"What?" Her smile faded. "There's a rule about not squirting the manager? You should've told me."

"Consider yourself told. When you finish Lena, I'll have you hold Snowflake while I give her a bath."

"Okay."

He caught the filly and picked up each of her feet before Jill finished. After handing Jill the lead, he removed the nozzle from the hose and turned the water on to a trickle. He worked it up Snowflake's leg, slowing when she became nervous.

Taking his time with a young horse came naturally. But it served the double purpose of keeping Jill occupied. He finished washing and used a sweat scraper to squeeze water from the filly's coat. He took a deep breath and said the words he dreaded.

"Okay. Put them in a stall till they dry." Molly began barking. "I'll go check on that."

He held himself to a walk. *Please, God, let it be Dotty.* When he saw her SUV, he let his breath out. He hurried around to the driver's door.

She smiled. "Sorry, I took so long. This sounded important."

"Thank God you're here."

"What is it?"

"Kevin's gone and I don't want to be alone with Jill. I think she has a crush on me."

Dotty burst out laughing. When she regained her composure, she glanced over his shoulder. "I'm glad you're here to help me with this, Cody. Hank's gone all day."

"No problem." He turned to Jill. "I need to give Dotty a hand at her place, so we'll have to call it a day. I'll see you tomorrow."

"Okay. You're sure there's nothing else you want me to do before I go?"

"You can put Lena's tack away. I have to get some stuff from the house. I won't leave till you're done."

"Okay."

"Come on, Dotty." He waited until they were out of earshot. "Thank you."

"I understand how she feels. You even make *me* hot and bothered."

He blushed. "I'm not trying to seduce anybody. Really, I'm not."

"You don't need to try. Look in the mirror."

"The way I look doesn't seem to effect Karlea."

She chuckled. "She watched you grow up. The rest of us don't have that buffer."

"Sometimes I wish she didn't either." He saw her brow furrow. "I mean ... sometimes she forgets I'm an adult."

"Oh. She's getting better."

"Yeah. Can you do me one more favor? Can you not tell Karlea about this?"

"Why not?"

"I just don't want her to say, 'I told you so.' She wanted me to talk down to Jill."

"You couldn't do that. That would make you like Bill. You're too nice. Okay. Mum's the word. Now, this is a temporary fix. Sooner or later you'll have to be alone with Jill."

"Tomorrow I'm trying Kate's plan."

"What's that?"

"I'll give Kate a kiss when she comes and goes. Make it look like there's something going on between us. Hopefully, that will be enough to discourage Jill."

"Sounds like Kate's plan alright. Sounds like her plan to get you into bed."

"Been there. Done that."

"You make it sound like past tense."

"It is. I didn't feel right about it. I'm not into Kate's kind of fun."

"My niece isn't looking for anything permanent or exclusive."

"Exactly."

"You're a good kid ... man, Cody. Karlea's lucky to have you."

IX

When Kate arrived the next day, she kissed Cody and grabbed the seat of his jeans.

"Quit that!" She raised her eyebrows. "Come on. I need to talk to you." He led her to the tackroom.

"What's up?"

He spoke in a whisper. "I came up with a better plan."

"I like my plan. But let's hear it."

"*You* talk to Jill about my girlfriend."

"I don't know anything about your girlfriend."

"You don't need to know anything. You just tell Jill how heartbroken you are because I'm head-over-heels in love with my North Dakota girlfriend. I can't think about anyone else."

"Heartbroken, huh? I don't feel heartbroken."

"You're telling me you can't lie to her?"

"I didn't say that. But I can't tell her I'm heartbroken with a straight face. I could tell her I'm disappointed. And *that* wouldn't be a lie."

"Fine. Just as long as she gets the message that there's no point in pursuing me. I'm taken."

"Okay. You might have come up with a pretty good plan there. She might only be looking for some great sex, not a boyfriend. Even if we kiss, she might think you play around. Telling her that you're a one-woman man should send the right message."

"Thanks. Let's go. I'll have Kevin help me and Jill help you."

"Brilliant!"

Cody growled and they returned to the barn aisle where Kevin and Jill had the two yearlings in the cross ties at opposite ends. Cody and Kate each picked up a saddle blanket and began "sacking" the young horses, rubbing the blanket over their bodies to get them used to equipment. Neither of the horses flinched. Cody had handled them all their lives.

While Kate harnessed the horse, she talked to Jill. She nodded toward the far end. "Must be tough working around *him* all day."

"Cody? Cody's nice."

"That's what I mean. He's *so hot.*"

Jill grinned. "Yeah. He is."

"That's what's so frustrating. A body like that and he won't even consider being unfaithful to his girlfriend back in North Dakota."

"He has a girlfriend?"

"Yeah. He never talked about her till I tried to get him into bed. I told him what she didn't know, wouldn't hurt her. Nothing doing. Cody's a one-woman man."

"Oh. Guess you got to admire him for it."

"Yeah. But I'm still frustrated. Hope she appreciates what a great guy she has. A body to kill for, nice, and faithful. Don't find many like that."

"No. And they're always taken."

***

After Kate's talk with Jill, Cody felt safe around her again. He still went to great lengths not to work alone with her, seeing no reason to take chances.

Though he kept himself busy, time seemed to drag, with Karlea's call the highlight of his day. He began to look forward to horse shows for the break in his routine. The other contestants called him "cowboy" because he refused to wear English riding clothes when not competing. He preferred to think of it as a compliment.

Both Kelsey and Celtic had improved. Kelsey won enough novice classes to elevate him to the working hunter division. By late July, Celtic needed just one more win to accomplish the same goal. Cody had his hopes pinned on a two-day show in Colorado. With his birthday the next day, he consider a win the ideal present.

After the halter classes, he changed to jeans and a western shirt. He, Hank, and Kate sat on lawn chairs in front of their stalls, visiting until their riding classes. He noticed them trying to suppress grins.

"What's the joke?"

Someone put their hands over his eyes.

"Guess who?" Kate said.

Cody knew the hands belonged to a woman. He inhaled and recognized the perfume.

"Karlea!" He leaped from his chair and they hugged for a very long time without a word. He failed to notice Kate's scrutiny. Finally, he regained his voice. "This is a shock."

"I've wanted to come watch you show all summer. I couldn't pass this up. Only an hour from Denver and I can help you celebrate your birthday. I spent two days spoiling my granddaughter before coming here."

"You didn't see the halter classes?"

"Just got here. How'd you do?"

"Kelsey placed fourth. Celtic won another beauty contest."

"She's a pretty girl."

"It's *so* great to see you."

They hugged again.

"Karlea," Hank said. "You're going to squeeze the stuffing out of the boy."

"Oh, he hates being called a boy."

"I call any male Kate's age or younger a boy."

Cody found another chair and placed it close to his. He finally noticed Kate eyeing him and managed to tone down his enthusiasm.

Hank spoke again. "I'll admit, I thought you were exaggerating when you told me what a horseman you had. But Cody's every bit as good as you said."

Karlea smiled at Cody. "He makes my life so much easier. I've felt like I was missing my right arm this summer. Jeff and Art can do the work, but I've had to tell them *everything*. They finally started doing the routine chores without being told. But if they see something that needs to be done, they ask me first. Cody just does it. I can't count the number of times I got out of bed in the morning to find him hard at work already."

Cody just smiled.

"Wish I could find someone like that," Hank said.

Kate laughed. "Dad, you're not as pretty as Karlea."

Karlea blushed while the rest of them laughed.

Hank agreed. "You got me there."

Cody and Karlea spent the rest of the day together. After supper, he drove her rental car to her motel. They shared another long hug, then talked far into the night. He loved the closeness and hated to give it up.

She finally said the obvious. "It's getting late."

"I know."

"I'd let you stay. But can you imagine the gossip that would cause?"

"Yeah."

"Tomorrow night we'll be home and we can stay together as long as we want."

He smiled and edged toward the door. "Okay."

"Just don't forget to come get me in the morning."

"Not likely. Would you do something for me?"

"What?"

He let his breath out. "Would you let me kiss you?"

"Huh?" She stared. "Why?"

"You're finally treating me like an adult. But I'm not sure you really mean it. You've kissed me on the cheek and the forehead. If you can share a real kiss with me, I'll be convinced."

She frowned. "I really do think of you as an adult."

He smiled at her in a way he never had before. She almost felt weak in the knees.

"Prove it."

"It's that important to you?"

"Yeah."

"It just doesn't seem like a very good idea, Cody."

He grinned. "Remember when I told you I'd be making other demands because I have to wear those goofy clothes?"

She half-smiled. "Now you're demanding a kiss?"

"Yeah. I can be *so unreasonable*."

She giggled. "Well, okay."

That smile returned as he approached and took her in his arms. She stiffened. The softness of his kiss surprised her. It broke down her defenses. She wrapped her arms around his shoulders and pressed her body into his. When he slipped his tongue into her mouth, she gripped his shirt.

After a very long kiss, she clung to him, now certain that her knees could not support her. He rubbed her back.

"Okay. Now I'm sure." *You'll never think of me as a boy again.*

"Uh-huh." She regained her strength, but did not move away. "What was *that*?"

"A pretty good kiss, if I do say so myself."

"I've *never* been kissed like *that*."

"Really? That's too bad. You deserve to be kissed like that. If you ever want another one, just let me know."

"Too many kisses like that and you won't be able to get me off you."

She heard the smile in his voice.

"I'm willing to risk it. Good night."

He left her staring at the door. She shook her head. "That's a *man*."

X

The next day Karlea helped Cody prepare for his classes and cheered him on. Kelsey finished fifth in the tougher working hunter division. Then Celtic won her class, also graduating from the novice division.

Cody drove Karlea's rental car, following Hank out of town. After he pulled onto the highway, she rested her hand on his arm. He glanced at her with a smile, then took her hand, resisting the urge to kiss it. *Don't come on too strong.*

He could see that she enjoyed the closeness almost as much as he did. They did not need to talk, just be together.

They reached the farm after dark. Hank and Kate helped unload horses, then equipment. When Kate had a moment alone with Cody, she slapped his rear end.

"Don't do anything I wouldn't do."

"That's *some* advice. Is there anything you wouldn't do?"

"Not much."

"Go home, Kate."

"I'm gone."

Karlea played with Molly until the horse trailer pulled away. "It's good to be home. Why'd you name her 'Molly'?"

"I didn't. She had a tag with her name on it. Her owners moved and couldn't take her with. Let's go in."

He grabbed their bags and followed her into the house.

She surveyed the livingroom. "I'm impressed. The place is pretty clean."

"So this was a surprise inspection."

"No."

She hugged him. He wanted to kiss her again, but resisted. *You don't want to seduce her. You want her to fall in love with you. Wait for her to ask.*

She sighed. "You as tired as I am?"

"Yeah."

"We can continue this in the morning."

He squeezed her. "Why not now? I enjoyed sleeping with you during that ice storm."

She stiffened. "I did too. But do you think that's a good idea? I understand that young men think about sex about ninety percent of the time."

"That's true." He chuckled. "But I've passed that stage. Now it's only fifty percent. I'll be fine."

"So I don't turn you on at all?"

"Oh, yeah. My body shouts, 'You're in bed with a beautiful woman!' But my brain says, 'Shut up. She's off limits.' My brain always wins."

She giggled. "You think I'm beautiful?"

"I can't be the first man who told you that."

"I always figured they were after my money."

"Some of them were. But most were after your body." He paused. "I know you're blushing."

She laughed harder and pulled away. "Okay. I'll sleep with you. I'll go change."

He finished before she did. When she saw his bare chest, she froze. "We had on a lot more clothes in April."

"It was cold."

"That's an awful lot of skin."

"So?"

"And I'm thinking about that kiss." He just grinned. "I might get fresh."

"Don't worry. I'm stronger than you are."

"Huh?"

"If you try to rape me, I can fight you off." She dissolved in laughter and he took advantage, scooping her up. She squealed. "Bedtime."

He deposited her on the sheets, still giggling. He joined her, fighting to control himself. Spontaneity in this location could prove dangerous. He kissed her nose.

"Cody, you really must be tired. You're not usually so playful."

"Partly that. But I'm just *so* happy to see you. This is a great birthday present. Thanks."

"You're welcome. Now, go to sleep."

***

Karlea woke feeling very aroused. She smiled and gazed at Cody, laying on his side next to her. Her eyes followed his muscular arm down to his hand, resting just below her navel.

That explains how I'm feeling. What a hunk! She surprised herself. *I haven't thought about Cody like that since I saw him naked.* Warmth spread throughout her body. *Karlea, control yourself. It must have been that kiss. He wanted me to think of him as an adult. Be careful what you wish for, Cody.*

She faced him. Without waking, he moved his hand to her hip, only slightly less stimulating. She stroked his shoulder, then summoned enough nerve to caress his chest. When he did not stir, she inhaled. She liked his scent. He smelled like a man. *Bill always smelled like an old ashtray.*

"What are you doing?"

She blushed, but managed an offhand reply. "Trying to wake you. It took long enough."

"Likely story."

"Happy birthday."

"Um-m. It certainly is. A beautiful woman in my bed."

"Stop that. What would you like to do today?"

"Chores. I've been gone two days."

"Most chores can wait. It's your birthday. Let's have some fun."

"We could stay in bed all day."

"Would you quit joking?"

"Okay. How about a trail ride?"

"Great. Where?"

"There are a bunch of riding trails in the White Mountains. It'll be a nice change of pace for you, riding through the pines."

"That sounds like fun. And tonight, I'll take you to a nice restaurant. Dotty suggested the Porter Mountain Steakhouse."

"That's a good place. Kate and I ate there once."

"Been on any more dates?"

He rolled his eyes. "Who has time?"

"You'd have time if you weren't such a slave driver."

"True. I'll think about it again after the boss moves in."

"You'd better."

He wrapped his arms around her and pulled her on top of him. "Help. Help. My boss is sexually harassing me."

She giggled. "I thought you were goofy because you were tired. But you're still goofy."

"It's the thin air."

"Not likely. You were always so straight-laced. What's going on?"

He frowned, hoping to convince her that he was pondering the question. He did not want her to move. Her legs had slipped down on either side of his body, an intimacy he wanted to maintain.

"Maybe this is me going wild. I always followed Mom and Dad's rules. I was *never* grounded."

"Never?"

"Never."

"Not even the first time you got drunk?"

He chuckled. "I passed out by nine, woke with a hangover by 11:30, and was home in bed by midnight. They never knew."

"Mr. Cheap Drunk."

"Guilty. Tell me how you met Hank and Dotty."

She smiled. "Dotty and I met in a hospital nursery. She was born the day before me. Our moms were friends. We were inseparable till my parents moved to North Dakota when we were fourteen. But every summer I spent a month in Montana and she spent a month with us. She was my maid of honor and I was her matron of honor."

"Dotty was married?"

"It lasted two years. She stayed with us for a couple months after her divorce. And, of course, Hank was always around too. About a year after we moved to North Dakota, I started babysitting you."

"Not *that* again. If you ever mention that again, I'll kiss you till you forget it."

She smiled and licked her lips. "Is that supposed to be a threat? You might find me talking constantly about it."

They both laughed. But when he rolled over with her, she finally noticed her suggestive position.

He eased her concern with a kiss on the nose. "Don't worry. I wouldn't kiss you like that here. Far too dangerous."

"I'm not sure I like thinking of you as an adult. It made me notice that you're all man."

His smile made her whole body feel warm again.

"Why, Karlea, are you horny?"

She wondered if he could read her mind. "Cody! You *have* gone wild. What would your mom say?"

"Hey! *You* convinced me to get away from home."

Her face turned a deeper shade of red. "This wasn't what I had in mind."

"I know. But it's good to see you thinking like a sexy, young woman instead of an old grandmother."

"I'm actually thinking about dating after I move."

"Good. If any of those guys do anything you don't like, just threaten them with me."

"I'll do that."

***

They enjoyed the day trail riding in Sitgreaves National Forest, returning home in time to do chores. The atmosphere at the steakhouse kept Cody from gazing into her eyes throughout the meal. He hoped that his love for Karlea did not show as much as he felt it.

I don't want to know when she has to leave. Only the moment mattered. When they returned home, he hugged her.

"Thanks for a wonderful day. It was special because you were here."

"You're a silver-tongued devil. Save that talk for the girls you're courting."

She could not see his grin. "You deserve some flattery."

A moment passed. "Would this be a good time for one of those kisses?"

"Give me a minute."

He needed the time to get his feelings in check. He could not afford to lose control and scare her. He placed one hand on the small of her back and stroked her neck with the other. The kiss left her clinging to him. But he felt tears on his neck.

"Karlea? I'm sorry. What's wrong?"

"It's not you. I'm scared."

"Of what?"

"You could get me to do anything. I just lose control."

"And you don't like that feeling."

"No. I like it. That scares me."

He kissed her forehead. "You know you can trust me."

"Yes."

"I promise, I won't try to get you to do anything. Let yourself enjoy the feeling." He paused. "I sure wasn't expecting this when I asked to kiss you. You respond like a sixteen-year-old virgin."

She pulled away, her cheeks red. "I'm going to tell your mom the things you're saying."

"And how'll you explain why I'm saying it?"

The red crept down her neck. "Never mind. You're right. I can't figure out why you make me feel like a school girl."

"You said you've never had a good kiss."

"Not even close."

"There must be a lot of other things you've missed. All kinds of new sensations to experience."

She smiled and he noticed her chest rise and fall faster. *Remember, you're not trying to seduce her. Back off.*

"Are you suggesting that you're the man to show me what I've missed?"

He stared at the floor, resisting the urge to shout, yes. "No. Just making an observation."

"It's an interesting observation."

"Ready for bed?"

"Together again?"

"It would be the perfect end to my birthday."

"What would?"

He studied the floor again, grinning. "Just the same as last night. Unless you think you can't be trusted."

"Probably not. But like you said, you're stronger than I am. One more night. Tomorrow, I use another bed."

"I can't expect to be spoiled all the time."

XI

Karlea spent the next day with Dotty, visiting and shopping. When they returned to Dotty's place in the afternoon, Karlea summoned the nerve to question her friend.

"Can I ask you some personal things? I don't really have anyone else to talk to."

"You'd better bring your personal problems to me. Is there a man?"

"Well, no, not really. I've just been thinking about men the past few months."

"It's about time. Any dates?"

"I want to wait till I move."

"Then what's so personal?"

"Ah-h, can a kiss take you all the way?"

Dotty blinked, and opened her mouth long before any words came. "Well, it's never happened to me. But maybe it could for you. From what you've said, Bill wasn't a very attentive lover."

"I guess not."

"And he was your only one?"

"Of course."

"But someone else has kissed you now. What was he doing with his hands?"

"He rubbed my back and my neck."

"Softly?"

Karlea smiled. "Very softly."

"That man knows what he's doing. Get him in bed."

"I-I c-couldn't do *that*." She shook her head. "No. That's not happening."

"Why not? You're not willing to have a fling? It has to be marriage?"

"I've thought about a fling. But not with him."

"Is he married?"

"No."

"The man wants you. What's the problem?"

"He doesn't want me. He was just being nice."

"Nice! The man who carries your groceries is being nice. The man licking your tonsils *wants you.* "

Karlea's voice dropped to a whisper. "No. You're wrong about that."

"Karlea, who *is* this guy?"

"It's Cody."

"Cody!"

"That's why you're wrong. I treated him like a kid for so long, he just wanted me to prove that I think of him as an adult. He said a kiss would convince him. That kiss felt better than sex ever did. He said I could ask for another, and I have."

"Uh-huh. Ask for more than a kiss."

"Dotty. I'm *his boss.* It would be sexual harassment."

"Not if he's interested."

"I told you. It was only a test. And he did it again, just to be nice."

"Uh-huh." She raised her eyebrows. "And he's got a body that won't quit. I've sworn off men and *I* get hot and bothered around him. And he hasn't kissed me."

"He's not interested, Dotty. He had me in the palm of his hand. I told him he could talk me into anything, and he didn't."

"That's pretty special. He's made the first move, now he's leaving the next to you."

"This is insane!" She covered her face. "What would I tell his mother?"

"Nothing! You just want to have a little fun. Why not start with the guy under your roof?"

She lowered her hands. "I'd be using him."

"If he wants to have some fun, then it's mutual. You just have to make sure he feels no pressure, that he's free to refuse with no hard feelings. Otherwise it *will be* sexual harassment."

"I can't do it with Cody. What happens when it's over? How can I move on to another guy when Cody lives with me? Way too complicated."

Dotty sighed. "You're going back to North Dakota in a couple days. Just don't rule it out. Try to think about him as a potential lover instead of your right hand man."

"I don't think I can stop myself."

***

Cody and Karlea shared one more long kiss before she left for Denver. That night, he lay awake, missing her intensely. He tried to console himself with the knowledge that she now saw him in a whole new light.

The following evening, he and Kate braved a monsoon to drive into Snowflake to eat. Fortunately, the rain stopped just before they reached La Cocina de Eva.

Kate studied him with a bemused smile.

He growled at her. "What're you staring at?"

"You look love sick."

"I do not."

"And Karlea isn't the love of your life. I'm not blind."

Cody opened his mouth, then closed it. His shoulders sagged. "Am I that obvious?"

"Just to me, because you told me you have a girlfriend in North Dakota."

"Please, don't tell anyone. Especially Karlea."

"I could see that she's clueless. Why don't *you* tell her?"

"So she can say she's not interested? I don't need that awkwardness in my life."

"Are you ever going to tell her?"

"Sure. First, I'm working on getting her to change how she thinks about me. I've made some progress. I'll work more on it after she moves."

"Then you'll tell her."

"Eventually."

"You're afraid to tell her."

"I'm afraid of the awkwardness."

"You're afraid of rejection. As long as you hide your love, she can't reject you."

He raised his glass to his mouth, then set it down without drinking. "You might be right."

"Nothing ventured. Nothing gained."

"I know. But we're talking about my whole life. I love Karlea. But I love my job too. I like it here. I even like showing the horses."

"You're kidding!"

"No. I actually enjoy it. If I blow it with Karlea, I'll ruin everything. Can you understand why I'm cautious?"

"No. It's not in my nature to be cautious. But I can see your point of view."

"Thanks."

"But speaking as someone who's been in the sack with you, treat her to a few of your encores and she'll follow you anywhere."

"If I wanted to seduce her, I could have done that already. I want her to love me."

"Define love."

"Something that outlasts the lust. Marriage. A lifetime commitment. What I feel for her."

"You *do* have it bad. Good luck."

"I think I need it."

XII

During the next few weeks, Kelsey scored two wins in the Open Working Hunter division. Celtic never finished higher than fourth. But she continued to win the beauty contests. The road trips helped eat up the time until Karlea's return.

September's cooler nights only served to heighten Cody's anticipation. When she told him to expect her on the twenty-third, he circled the day on the calender. He resisted crossing off each passing day, thinking it too obvious.

Because she would not come alone, he prepared himself to hold off on the kind of reunion he wanted. On the tenth, she informed him that his parents and Ben would make the trip with her.

The night before their arrival, he lay awake thinking of her. On the twenty-third, he became agitated waiting for her call, telling him they had turned south at Holbrook. It came just before one.

He called Hank, Dotty, Kevin, and Jill, who he had recruited to help. He planned to have horses and furniture unloaded by nightfall.

After a round of hugs and introductions, everyone set to work unloading horses. Cody left Kevin and Jill to empty and clean the trailer while everyone else tackled the moving van. After a supper prepared by Dotty, the extra help departed, leaving a house far more crowded than it had been that morning.

Cody surveyed the extra furniture and bodies. "This will take some getting used to."

"Your bachelor days are over," Allen said.

"It was nice while it lasted."

Nancy saw an opening. "Kate seems like a nice girl."

Cody and Karlea exchanged knowing smiles.

He tried to explain delicately. "Mom, Kate's a good friend. But she's not wife material. If I just wanted a good time, I'd go out with Kate."

"Oh."

"And I didn't come down here to look for a wife anyhow."

"I know. But you might stumble onto one."

He grinned. "Anything's possible."

Karlea laughed. "I'll try to give him time to date. But he's taking the next couple days off to show you the sights. You can't leave without seeing the Grand Canyon."

He wanted to spend that time with Karlea. "But there's so much work to do."

"Ben can help me. He can see the sights when he comes back for Christmas. This is the only pay Nancy and Allen are getting for all their work. And you need the time off."

Cody nodded, feeling guilty. He and Karlea would spend every day together. His parents's visits would be few. *I need to quit taking them for granted.* "You're right. We can do that tomorrow. But before they leave, I want them to see the Salt River Canyon too. I love that drive."

***

Alone at last.

Cody feared that the privacy would be too much for him. Karlea sat by the kitchen table, making a list of things to do. He wanted nothing more than to wrap his arms around her and kiss her the way she liked. He tore his gaze from her, afraid that she would look up and see the love in his eyes.

The phone rang, providing a welcome distraction. Hank wanted to talk to Karlea. Cody listened to her end of the conversation while he spread jam on his bagel.

"Hi, Hank ... They just left ... Tonight? ... I don't know. I have an awful lot to do ... Yes, I do deserve a break ... Okay ... Six is fine. I'll see you then." She disconnected. "Hank wants to take me to dinner tonight."

"A date?"

"Lord, I hope not."

Cody could not hide his smile. "I thought you liked Hank."

"I do, in a big brother sort of way. I'm afraid he wants more than that."

"Kate says he's had the hots for you for years."

"*Wonderful.* I have to nip this in the bud. Being subtle all these years obviously hasn't worked. I'll just have to break his heart. But I'll go out with him before I do."

"Might as well get a free meal."

"No. I'm being nice."

"I see. Well, I'd better finish this and get to work before I get fired."

She rolled her eyes. "You're the only slave driver here."

***

Cody spent the evening unable to concentrate on anything. He felt jealous for no good reason. He finally forced himself to clean his bathroom, a task he had been avoiding. He heard the front door open as he finished scrubbing the floor. He greeted Karlea, wiping his hands on a towel.

She gazed at his bare chest and cut-off jeans. "What were you doing?"

"Cleaning my bathroom. I put it off long enough. How'd it go?"

"He was disappointed. And he tried to change my mind. But he finally accepted my decision. It could have been worse."

"Glad he didn't throw a fit."

She giggled and wrapped her arms around his neck. He placed his hands on her waist and pushed her back.

"I'm all sweaty."

"I don't care. I need a hug."

He obliged her. "Um-m. You smell better than I do."

"I should hope so. Although I don't mind a sweaty man who doesn't smell like an old ashtray."

After a moment, she kissed his shoulder, sending sensations throughout his body.

"What was that for?"

"Could I have another of those kisses?"

"You're getting addicted to those."

"Very funny. It's been two months since you kissed me."

"Seems longer."

He obliged her, using his hands to enhance the experience. This time she did not become weak-kneed. Instead, her fingers massaged his back like a happy cat. He tried to resist the added stimulation, but finally failed. He pushed away just a few inches and rested his forehead against hers.

"I'm sorry," she said.

"That's my line."

"I asked for the kiss. You're a man. You were bound to get turned on, the way I've been teasing you."

"You've been teasing me?"

"As if you hadn't noticed."

"Define teasing."

"Bill said that any time a woman touches a man, she's teasing."

Cody scowled. *He really screwed her up.* "So you've been teasing me all my life."

"It doesn't apply to boys. But when you grew up and I kept treating you like a boy, I was teasing. I think I did it just to spite Bill. He really yelled at me about it. After he died, I figured he couldn't stop me."

"What else have you been doing to tease me?"

"Asking you to live with me was a big come on. Kissing you, not just the good ones. And sleeping with you. And now I pushed you even farther. I might as well wear a T-shirt that says, 'Take me!' I've been shameless."

"Did you intend any of those things as come ons?"

"Of course not. But I knew that's what they were."

"I didn't take any of them that way. If you'll recall, some of those things were my ideas. So, you might say I was teasing you."

Karlea giggled. "A man can't tease a woman."

"I'll prove you wrong."

"How?"

"The goal of teasing is sex. Right?"

"That or frustration."

"True. Want some sex?"

She blushed. "No."

"I think I can tease you into changing your mind."

Her body quivered. "You want to make love to me?"

Yes! "No. I want to frustrate you." He grinned.

"Go on."

"I'll bet that I can do it without kissing you below the collar bone. And I won't touch anything I haven't touched before."

"And the point of this demonstration?"

"At the risk of making you mad, Bill totally messed you up about the chemistry between men and women. I want you to question what you've learned."

"Why?"

"It'll be good for you."

"Okay. Go ahead."

He began by backing away, just smiling and undressing her with his eyes. Her face turned very red. He circled behind her, wrapped his arms around her waist, and simply breathed in her ear. She writhed and moaned in his arms. When he kissed her neck, she shrieked.

He stopped and helped her relax. "Deep breaths. You got pretty excited there."

"I like it. I've never felt anything like that. I want more."

"You're in no condition to make that decision. You're high on endorphins. Think about it when you have a clear head."

After some time, she sighed. "Good thing one of us has a clear head. You were right. I wish Bill had known how to tease a woman."

Cody sighed. *I guess he had a lot of shortcomings in the bedroom. I wonder if he didn't know or if he just didn't care.* Based on his experience with Bill Johnson, he suspected the latter.

XIV

Within a week, Karlea had another date. Although Cody joked about it, he felt intense jealousy. *If I don't tell her how I feel soon, someone else might. I've had her to myself for so long, I've started taking it for granted. She's a beautiful woman.*

She had described this man as a friend of Hank's from Show Low she had met numerous times through the years. Cody did not know him, but he seemed polite when he came to the door promptly at 6:30.

Cody immediately disliked him. He resisted the urge to comment, just telling her to have a good time. He set to work cleaning the house, the only thing he could accomplish in his state of mind.

Just past 7:30, the phone interrupted him. He recognized Karlea's cell number on the caller ID. "What's wrong?"

"Could you come get me, please?"

"Right away. What'd he do?"

"He wouldn't keep his hands off me."

"Where are you now?"

"In the lady's room."

"Stay there. What restaurant?"

"Stockmen's."

"I'll be there in twenty minutes. I'll call from the parking lot. If I come in, I'll probably hit him."

"He's probably gone. I dumped ice water in his lap."

"Good girl. I'll be right there."

He pulled on a T-shirt and ran to the pickup. *I will hit him if I see him.*

Two miles out of Taylor, he checked his speedometer. Eighty in a sixty-five mile per hour zone. He moderated his speed, then his anger, before reaching Show Low.

Karlea came as soon as he called. He simply squeezed her hand and turned east on Deuce of Clubs toward home. When they neared the farm, he kissed the hand.

"You can always count on me."

"I know. Thank you."

He helped her out of the pickup, then wrapped his arm around her shoulders as they walked to the house. In the livingroom, she began crying. He held her, kissing her forehead again and again.

"You're safe. I won't let anyone hurt you."

"I asked him to stop. Then I demanded. He wouldn't listen. I didn't want him to touch me like that. I swear I wasn't teasing him."

"I know you weren't. Next time I see him, I'll teach him some manners."

"Don't get into trouble for me."

"There won't be any witnesses."

"I knew I could count on you. I just couldn't ask him to take me home. I was afraid to be alone with him."

"You did the smart thing. Do you need me to chaperone your dates?"

"I'm through dating. At least till I come up with a better strategy. This was way too scary. I think he expected sex tonight."

"That's pretty common. A lot of people believe every date should include sex."

She shuddered. "I didn't know that. Now, I *really* don't want to date. Sex with a complete stranger doesn't appeal to me. I feel so safe with you. Will you sleep with me tonight? I may have nightmares."

"Anytime."

***

The next day, Cody told Karlea that he had an errand. He drove to Hank's place. Finding him alone in the stable, he wasted no time.

"We need to talk."

"Something wrong?"

"Karlea had a date with your friend, Roger, last night."

"Good God! Is she okay?"

Cody had expected Hank to defend his friend. He frowned. "Just scared. He pawed her and I had to go into Show Low and bring her home."

"If she'd asked me, I would've told her to stay clear of him."

"Next time you see him, tell him to stay clear of me. He needs to learn manners, and he won't like my teaching methods."

Hank grinned. "I'll tell him. After I knock him on his tail. We'll teach him not to mess with *our* Karlea. Maybe she's right about me. I feel like a protective big brother."

Cody liked Hank a little more than he had just a day earlier. "I expected an argument. Thought you and Roger were buddies."

"We are. But he's a womanizer. Married twice and never thought to stop dating either time. I usually stay out of Kate's love life, but I told her to steer clear."

"And she listened?"

Hank laughed. "Yeah. The warnings come so few and far between, she notices. Tell Karlea to ask me before she goes out with anyone else."

"She's sworn off dating for a while. But I'll tell her. I don't like how I felt last night."

"I guess she has an older brother and younger brother in you and I. But we can't protect her all the time."

"We can sure try."

XV

During the next few days, Karlea stayed close to Cody in public places. If a seemingly unattached man approached, she nearly hid behind him. If the man took special interest in her, she held Cody's arm until the threat departed.

But at home she kept her distance. Their physical contact dwindled to one quick hug a day. No more kisses or intimate talks. Cody wondered if she had sworn off all men, including him. He tried to gather the nerve to ask her about it. He had almost convinced himself when he noticed her distraction. *I won't bother her when she has something on her mind.*

But she seemed distracted all week. He finally asked.

"Is something bothering you?"

"Ah. Um-m. Ah. Well, I just have something on my mind."

"Did I do something wrong?"

"No! No. Why would you say that?"

"Because you've kind of been avoiding me."

"Oh." She frowned. "I'm sorry. I didn't realize it." She hugged him. "You didn't do anything wrong. I'm just preoccupied."

"Okay. Do you want to talk about what's bothering you?"

She stiffened. "Thank you. Maybe after awhile. But right now, this is something I need to work through myself."

He nodded and stroked her hair. "Okay. Just remember, I'm here for you."

"Oh, I know. Never forget how much I appreciate that."

***

Between that conversation and Karlea making a point to hug him more often, Cody relaxed. However, when another week passed, he began to wonder about the kisses. *She really likes those. Why hasn't she asked me to kiss her?*

He sat in his favorite chair one evening, thinking about that while pretending to read a magazine. *She's still distracted. She hasn't turned a page in her book in five minutes.*

Karlea closed it, then fidgeted for a moment. "Cody, I need to talk to you about something."

"Sounds important."

"It is. I've been thinking about this for a while, trying to figure out the right way to say it. No matter how I word it, it sounds bad."

He set the magazine aside. "Then just say it."

"Well, first I want you to know that no matter how you answer, it won't effect your job. One thing has nothing to do with the other. You have to know that you're totally free to refuse. *I'm* not even sure if I should suggest this. So, if you don't think it's a good idea, I'm totally okay with it."

He frowned. "O-kay."

"Um-m. Would you like to have ... Would you like to ... go to ... Are you interested in ... sex ... with me?"

His jaw dropped and he felt dizzy. His brain failed him. Then thoughts began to form. *I expected this some day. In the distant future. After I tell her I love her. She's only lived here a month. I'm not ready!*

Karlea began to fidget. "I'm sorry. This was a bad idea. Please forget I mentioned it."

He shook his head to clear it. "Wait a minute! I didn't say it was a bad idea. I'm just shocked. You can't drop a bombshell like that and just withdraw the question. The words can't be unsaid."

"I'm sorry."

"Don't be. I'm flattered that I'm the man you trust that much. I know from the way you've been distracted, it was a really tough decision for you. I want to take some time to think about your offer."

"You do?" She leaned back in her chair. "How much time?"

"I'll let you know before the evening is over. But I'm not interested in a one night stand."

"Oh, neither am I. But we would have to keep it quiet. Our families would about flip if they heard about it. And no strings attached. I'm not looking to rope a husband."

"Doesn't matter. I'm not afraid of marriage. I'm going to my room to think about this for a while." He strolled to his room, closed the door, then beat his bed with a pillow. "This isn't what I wanted."

He sank to the bed. *What did you expect, moron? You've been seducing her since July.*

"I didn't mean to. I wanted her to know how much I love her."

The damage had been done. Karlea just wanted an affair. He needed to know if it was his fault. Composing himself, he wandered back to the livingroom. She stopped pacing.

"I have a question. Have I seduced you into this?"

"No. No. I was thinking about a relationship long before you kissed me. But I couldn't find anyone who I trusted enough to let myself go. I had a blind spot where you were concerned, even after you kissed me." She forced a smile. "That babysitting thing. If I hadn't known you for so long, the kisses *might* have seduced me. But when you came to my rescue, I finally put aside your age. I wanted you that night. I've been trying for the past two weeks to get the nerve to ask you."

"Which explains why you couldn't tell what was on your mind."

"Exactly." She bit her lip. "There's something else I have to tell you. I rarely enjoyed sex. I'm not interested in a one night stand, but I could lose interest in a hurry."

"Oh, if I do this, you'll enjoy it. And you certainly won't lose interest."

She blushed. "The way you kiss, I'm guessing you're right. One other thing. If we start this, we need to agree that either one of us can end it at any time with no hard feelings. I mean, not without an explanation. But our friendship and our working relationship need to be more important to both of us."

"Easier said than done, but I agree. I need to think some more."

He returned to his bedroom and sighed. *I don't want a secret affair with Karlea.* He wanted a ring on her finger for the whole world to see.

But this will give her time to fall in love with me. I won't have to worry about her dating someone else. Don't be an idiot. The woman you love wants to make love to you.

"What am I waiting for? I need a shower."

***

Karlea read the same line in her book for the fourth time. She sighed and stared down the hallway. She had been so afraid to ask, afraid that he would refuse and quit his job. *But he's actually considering it.*

The thought made her feel warm all over. *Maybe Dotty was right. Maybe he was trying to tell me that he was interested.*

No one could ever know about this. *Well, maybe Dotty. She won't betray the confidence. But if his parents or my kids find out about it ...* She shuddered.

Cody's return interrupted her thoughts. Her heart raced. Only a towel covered him. He stopped six feet from her and dropped that. She gasped, her face crimson.

"What ... happened to my shy farm boy?"

He licked his lips and barely whispered. "Tonight, you made us equals. I was never shy with my girlfriends."

"Now I'm your girlfriend?"

"Sounds good to me."

He held out his hand. When she took it, he helped her up. He caressed her cheek and neck, then unfastened the top button of her blouse.

She moved to help him. "I'm sorry I'm so slow."

He grasped her hands and kissed both. "If I undress you, I'm not in a hurry. It's for your enjoyment. It's foreplay." He continued, noticing her surprise.

"That's what they mean by foreplay?"

It would have been funny if she had not been serious. *How could a woman who was married that long be so innocent?*

He pushed the blouse off her shoulders, then pulled her close for a short kiss. Before he finished, he had removed her bra. His hands began to shake.

She noticed and held them between hers. "Are you afraid?"

"No. Just a little case of nerves. This is a big change for us."

"A huge change. Are you sure you want to do this?"

"I've wanted to do this for a long time. The nerves will pass."

"This is what you were trying to tell me with the kisses? You're attracted to me. That bit about thinking of you as an adult was a little white lie?"

"No. You needed to think of me as an adult before we could get here. So that was my first goal. Getting you to think about sex was just a fringe benefit of using kisses to accomplish my goal."

"So you *were* trying to seduce me."

"That wasn't really my intention. But I guess I knew it could happen. I'm sorry."

"I don't mind. I still trust you more than any other man. You've taken care of me in so many ways. I know you'll do the same in bed."

"I promise."

He traced her lips, then let his fingers glide down to her breast.

She jerked away. "I-I'm sorry. No one's ever touched me like that."

"But you were *married*. He never touched your breast?"

"No."

He shook his head. "Okay. We'll save that for another time. I don't want to shock you too much. What kind of foreplay are you used to?"

"Well, he undressed me. But it would have been more exciting if he hadn't acted impatient. And he kissed me, but not like you do."

Cody waited for more, but there was none. *Plenty of men treat prostitutes better than he treated her. What was she to him, a sex toy?* He hugged Karlea to hide his anger. "I'll just do what I've done before. That will get you plenty excited."

He kissed her while he finished removing her clothes, then carried her down the hall to her bedroom. He kicked the door closed to keep Molly out. After he lay Karlea on the blankets, he paused.

"Do you want me to use protection?"

She giggled. "It's not like I can get pregnant."

He saw no reason to lecture her on the other reasons for safe sex. Neither of them needed to worry about catching anything from the other. He liked the thought of having nothing between them. When she reached for the light, he stopped her.

"No. I want to see you when I make love to you."

"I've always made love in the dark."

"You'll be doing lots of new things."

He concentrated his kisses on her neck, the quickest way to arouse her. He fought to control himself, wanting her to enjoy this as long as possible.

When he gave in, he was astonished by the physical effort that he put into their first time. He remembered nothing else like it.

Karlea covered her face, gasping. After her breathing slowed, she took her hands away, grinning. "I'm not just saying this. That was the best ever!"

He lay beside her, struggling to control his emotions. "I believe you."

"I didn't know it could last so *long!*"

He pulled her into his arms and kissed the top of her head. He wiped his eyes before speaking again. "My love, that was a quickie."

She tensed. "It can last longer than that?"

"Much."

"Oh-h. I can't wait! Same time next week?"

"Next week?"

"Too soon?"

He laughed, his emotions in check. "Do you really want to wait till next week?"

"No. That was great. I could do it again tomorrow. Could we?"

"Sure we can. But I'm not done with you tonight."

She shuddered. "Oh, my."

"Before we continue, we need to get some things straight. First, forget everything you learned from Bill. He was a very poor teacher. And we are giving our bodies to each other. I'll eventually touch or kiss most of yours. You need to get used to my touch. Feel free to do the same with me."

"Okay."

"I'll go slow."

"Okay."

When he placed his palm on her belly, she gasped. After a moment, she relaxed and smiled.

"You did this to me before, but you were asleep at the time."

"My subconscious at work. Where should this hand go next? You be my guide."

She giggled and tentatively moved his hand.

XVI

The next morning, Karlea lay in bed staring at Cody. Thoughts cluttered her mind. *I can't believe what I've been missing. Nancy would hate me if she knew. He's so good at this. Deb would throw a fit if she knew. I enjoyed sex for the first time in my life last night. What they don't know won't hurt them.*

She began kissing his chest, working her way up to his neck. He smiled and wrapped his arms around her.

"Good morning, my love."

"Morning. I need a pet name for you."

"Why?"

"It just seems appropriate."

"How about 'stud?' I like that."

She giggled. "Well, it fits in some ways. But a stud is supposed to reproduce. That's wasted on me."

"Technicalities."

"I could call you 'incredible'."

"Better wait till the newness wears off."

"You're probably right. I'm still giddy. The first time was great. The second time, even better. I think you've created a monster. Watch out."

"I don't mind. I like making love to you."

"Even if I'm inept at foreplay."

He touched her lips. "I like your inexperience. I never thought I'd need to teach you. I feel privileged to be the man who's finally treating you right."

Her eyes glistened and her lip quivered, but she nodded. "Bill loved me, but he didn't know how to make love to me. Our marriage could have been so much better. He was twenty years older. He'd been married before. Why didn't he know these things?"

He stroked her hair. "He probably never had a woman tell him to do better or go without."

"Did you?"

"Sure. My first girlfriend. When I followed her advice, I liked the results."

"How many girlfriends have you had?"

"Let me think." He frowned and pretended to count on one hand, then the other, then back to the first.

Her eyes widened. "Cody!"

"Not counting Kate, three."

"Three! You let me think there were dozens. Wait a minute. If you're not counting Kate, how many more aren't you counting?"

"I'm not counting her because she was my one and only one night stand. The other three were anywhere from a few months to a little over a year."

"So I can expect this to be over in a year?"

He kissed her softly. "No. I'm more mature and you're not a teenaged girl. We're not going to break up because I didn't notice your new haircut or because I'm spending too much time with my pretty lady boss."

"Really! You broke up over me?"

"My last girlfriend. She was jealous because I stayed after work. I figured you needed me more than she did."

"You've always spent so much time just listening to me. Before Bill died, you let me vent. Afterward, you were my shoulder to cry on. You're my rock."

He hugged her. "Glad I could help. Well, sex is great, but you still need me to work too. I'd better get to it."

***

Cody poured coffee after morning chores. Karlea approached from the rear, wrapped her arms around him and began unsnapping his shirt. He drank even as she unbuckled his belt.

"Hot again?"

She just giggled. He turned and kicked off his boots, then let her finish undressing him. The previous night's activity had dulled his libido just enough to allow some very intense foreplay. He pushed her robe off and caressed whatever he wanted to. He lifted her. When she grabbed his shoulders, he wrapped her legs around him.

She frowned. "Don't drop me."

"Never happen."

"What are you doing?"

He smiled and maneuvered her into position. She gasped and wrapped her arms around his neck for the most intense experience of her life.

When her feet touched the floor again, she hid her face against his heaving chest, unable to fight the tears.

"What's wrong?"

"Nothing. My senses are just overloaded. Every time I think it can't get better, it does."

"One of these times it'll be just so-so. Try not to be too disappointed."

"Never happen. I can't compare this to anything I've ever done. So-so with you is great compared to what I had before. It was the same every time. Flat on my back. A few kisses. Most of the time, I'd lay there and wait for him to get done because I felt nothing. I didn't mind that it was only every week or two."

"So how'd you ever convince yourself to try someone else?"

"Because there were a handful of times when I felt something. I knew it was supposed to feel good. I'd heard other women talk about it."

"Now you know. Next time, I'll let you on top. I think you'll like that."

She smiled and kissed his neck. "How often can we keep doing this?"

"We still have work to do. And we have to sleep some time. But I'm willing to give up my TV and reading time."

"Me too. I'll even give up some of my work time."

"If you want to cut into my work time, you'll have to check with my boss."

"Don't worry. You have her wrapped around your little finger."

"That's not all she's wrapped around."

She licked her lips. "We'll call this one of your chores."

"The kind I like."

"I'll say, um-m, I need your muscles. Or I need you to help me with something."

He laughed. "And both would be true."

***

For the next week only a lingering sense of guilt interfered with Cody's ecstasy. He had wanted to fulfill all of Karlea's fantasies as her husband. But he had never seen her happier. He placed her happiness above everything. Guilt. Sleep.

And he *was* tired. Sex lasted well into the night. Time during the day that had once been reserved for relaxation now involved exertion. He needed rest, but would not refuse her.

Each day she made him lunch, then they made love. He usually finished his lunch with her lips somewhere on his body. He had encouraged her to experiment, learning new ways to excite him. As he grew wearier, he needed the help.

After yet another lunchtime session, Karlea savored the moment, then leaned down and kissed him. No response. He seemed to be asleep. *No one can fall asleep that fast.*

"Cody."

Still no response. She lay beside him and rubbed his chest hard. Nothing.

"You're sure tired for the middle of the day."

She studied him a little longer. *Of course he's exhausted. Rullah doesn't do it this often. And the only other thing Rullah has to do is eat. You still expect Cody to do all his work AND you're cutting into his sleeping time. Get a little self-control.* She sighed. *I suppose I could enjoy this a little less often.*

She left him sleeping while she tended to some neglected housework.

***

Cody woke to the aroma of food. It smelled like beef roast with all the trimmings. That would be a nice change from the sandwiches and frozen pizzas they had subsisted on since beginning their affair. Karlea had lost interest in cooking.

I hope we're not getting company. He smiled. She would have warned him. He glanced at the alarm clock, then bolted out of bed. Seven PM. He looked around the room for his clothes, but remembered he had left them in the kitchen. When he opened the bedroom door, he nearly ran into her.

"Why'd you let me sleep so long? I'm way late for chores."

"I did chores. You needed rest."

"Oh."

"I was just coming to wake you for supper."

"There was stuff I should have gotten done this afternoon."

"It can wait. You're exhausted. I need to give you a break. You can sleep in your own bed tonight. Get dressed. I'll put supper on the table."

"Okay."

Feeling a little disoriented, he dressed and joined her in the kitchen. They ate in silence through his first helping.

He smiled as he speared another slice of the roast. "This is great."

"Thank you. I'm afraid I've been neglecting everything but sex lately."

"You didn't hear me complaining."

"You wouldn't. You had to keep giving till you passed out before I realized how much I was asking of you."

"I passed out?"

"You fell asleep really fast. I was thoughtless."

"No. You're like a starving person who finally gets to eat. And you've been maintaining the same schedule I have. I figured you'd get tired sooner or later. I'm just glad I didn't have a horseshow this week."

"I haven't been keeping the same schedule." She stared at her plate. "I'm sorry. I've been sneaking naps when you were out working."

He laughed. "You've been cheating!"

"Yes. You can sleep tonight. I'll leave you alone. Starting tomorrow, I'll try to be satisfied with once at night and once at lunch."

"I can live with that. I wasn't sure I could survive the pace we've been keeping. I dozed off on the tractor yesterday. Gave myself a real scare."

"You have to learn to say 'no' to me."

"I've never liked saying 'no' to you."

"Oh, my." Karlea felt like her eyes had been opened. "How could I have missed that? When I asked you to move down here, to show, to make love to me, you couldn't refuse me."

"No."

"I'm sorry. I should have figured that out. You're so dedicated. I asked too much. If I had known, I never would have asked you to start an affair."

"No, you didn't ask too much. I'm happy I did all those things, even showing. And the sex. Remember, I wanted it too. And it's the best I've ever had."

"Now you're just being nice."

He took her hand. "No, really. For one thing, this is my first adult relationship. We're both trying to give, not just get. And you're so enthusiastic. You're so willing to experiment. When I thought I was too tired, you convinced me I wasn't."

She smiled and gazed at him from under her eyelashes until her practical side took over. "Still, if you don't take care of yourself, you can't take care of me. You could have gotten hurt yesterday."

"Yeah. I just hated to discourage you. You've had enough of that in your life."

"I've had a great life."

He scowled. "In some ways. But, remember, I knew Bill. I heard him put you down. I can't forget that. And now I know that he didn't take care of you in other ways."

She cleared her throat. "I know I have selective memory when it comes to my marriage. I remember my great step-sons and my beautiful daughter. I remember that he bought me everything I ever wanted and encouraged me to raise the kind of horses I wanted when everyone else laughed at me. I've pushed the bad stuff out of my mind. Plenty of women have it worse."

"I'm sorry. I shouldn't have brought it up."

"No. It's okay for you to give me a reality check sometimes. Bill wasn't a saint."

"I feel better when you remember that."

"Now." She smiled. "We need to live in the real world. We can't spend the whole day on sex. We have to work and interact with others."

"We're just lucky no one interrupted us."

"I never even thought of that. I probably wouldn't have been so enthusiastic if I had."

"How do you plan to deal with next weekend?"

"The Scottsdale show? I'll get a room. You can come visit me."

"We'll say I'm using your shower."

"Good plan. Ready for dessert?"

He licked his lips. "What did you have in mind?"

"Cody! You're resting tonight. I baked a chocolate cake."

"You were busy this afternoon."

"About time."

When they finished, he helped her clear the table.

She hugged him. "Now, you sit and relax or go back to bed. I won't disturb you either way. Sleeping in your own bed will guarantee that."

He hesitated. "Okay. I guess I'll go to bed. I'm still tired."

"Good night."

"Night."

Karlea watched him go to his room and close the door. *Something doesn't feel right. But what could be wrong? I'm just giving him the chance to get the rest he needs.*

In his own room.

She knocked on his door and entered without waiting for a reply. Cody sat on the bed, staring at the floor.

"Would you rather sleep with me?" He nodded. "I'm sorry. I thought you'd like your space."

"I don't just like making love to you. I like being with you."

"You wanted to sleep with me even before we had sex."

"Yeah. This felt like you didn't want me without the sex."

"Oh, I'm so bad at this. I think you're the best thing that ever happened to me. Remember that when I'm thoughtless."

She wrapped her arms around him and he sighed.

"I'm probably over-sensitive because I'm so tired."

"Come. I'll try not to disturb you when I join you."

"I don't think you can."

XVII

Dotty destroyed their best-laid plans when she decided that since this would be the last horse show of the year, she should go along. She volunteered to ride with Karlea and share the expense of her hotel room. Karlea looked at Cody and shrugged.

Later, crossing the Mogollon Rim on Highway 277, she decided the time had come to enlighten Dotty. "Cody's coming to our room to shower tonight and tomorrow night."

"No problem."

"So I'll need you to get lost for an hour or so."

Dotty gaped, sputtered, then finally laughed. "You did it! You actually jumped his bones!"

"I must have. I've done things with him I never dreamed of."

"You're priceless, Karlea. And I can see you're having fun. I'm so happy for you. You deserve a man who knows how to please a woman."

"You had no way of knowing that was Cody."

"I made an educated guess. He's sweet and he thinks the sun rises and sets on you. He's bound to take that into the bedroom. Didn't I tell you he was interested?"

"You did. But I shocked him. I think he believed it would never happen."

"Doesn't matter. He's in your bed. Tell me all the juicy details. You've never had anything quite so exciting to talk about."

"I shouldn't kiss and tell."

"Spill it. I've told you enough."

Karlea grinned. "He's incredible. Gentle and slow. And very thorough. Casual sex with him feels more loving than what passed for making love in my marriage. If I'd known what I was missing, it wouldn't have lasted."

"You would've divorced Bill?"

"No. I would've told him to do better or go without, and he would have showed me the door."

"Probably. Tell me more."

"I'm making up for lost time. He nearly killed himself trying to keep me satisfied."

Dotty laughed. "You don't have to embellish."

"I'm not. He passed out from exhaustion before I realized how much I was asking of him. I went back and counted. That first week we made love twenty-nine times."

"Twenty-nine? Why, Karlea, you wild woman. You could have killed a man in worse shape. How did you accomplish anything that week?"

"I didn't. I took naps when I should have been cooking and doing housework. But it never occurred to me that he might be tired too. I still expected him to do his chores. We've cut back to twice a day, so he gets his rest."

"It's nice having a young man. They have so much energy."

"Um-m. But I appreciate things that have nothing to do with his age. He knows so much more about sex than I do." She glanced at Dotty. "He says I acted like a virgin. I trust him. I know he won't tell any of his friends what we're doing. He's so thoughtful. He likes sleeping with me, even if we don't make love. I know he hates the way Bill treated me. But he usually just says Bill didn't know any better."

"He's being generous. Or very tactful. Bill neglected you."

"He gave me everything I ever wanted."

"Everything but love and affection. He was a cold man."

"You're right. But it was just the way he was raised. He didn't know any better."

"I suppose. Let's not dwell on the past. The present is so much better. You were so naive, Cody must have shocked you a time or two."

"Um-m. I've learned so much. He's very thorough."

"You already said that. The most unusual place you did it?"

Karlea grinned. "In the kitchen."

"On the table?"

"No. He just stood there and held me, like extremely close dancing."

"Oh-h. I'm jealous. You know, you're glowing."

"I doubt that I've ever felt better."

"But ..."

"I feel a little guilty."

"Are you still worried about his age?"

"No. Cody's an adult. I don't feel like I seduced him. He actually worried that he seduced me."

"So why are you feeling guilty?"

"I felt kind of guilty when I finally realized that he can't say 'no' to me. But, like you said, he wanted it too." She sighed. "I just feel like he deserves better. He should have a wife and family, not a lover with grandchildren."

"Some day he will. For now, you're both having fun. You adore each other." Dotty frowned. "There's something else bothering you."

"I believe I should have a license to have this much fun."

"That's between you and your conscience. But you didn't have this much fun when you did have a license."

"At least you didn't say I have no reason to feel guilty. Thanks for being the person I can trust with this."

"In other words, keep my mouth shut."

"Right. My kids and his parents can't find out about this. If anyone else finds out, they'll think he's just my 'boy toy.' Cody's words. It won't matter that he's a competent manager and a terrific trainer. That would really bother me."

"Unfortunately, it's true. Just look at the way I reacted. And I know how great he's been to you all these years."

"Exactly. Other people don't know what he's meant to me. They just see that great body."

"You can count on me. I won't tell a soul."

***

A week later, while working in the stable, Karlea heard Cody's voice.

"Karlea, could you help me?"

She left the stall, closing the door, and looked up and down the aisle for him. "Where are you?"

"In the tackroom."

"Be right there."

She hung the halter she carried on a peg outside, opened the door, and froze.

Cody stood by the sofa, wearing his shirt, unbuttoned, and socks. Nothing else. She just managed to keep a straight face.

"Nice outfit. What did you need?"

He gave her his sexiest smile. "You already rode the horse. Time to ride the cowboy." She laughed. "And close the door. This outfit's a little cool for November."

She obeyed and removed her jacket. "This is a surprise. I'm usually the one to make the first move."

"Exactly. I don't want you to start thinking you're imposing on me. Like, oh, no. Here comes Karlea and she's randy *again*."

She chuckled while leaning against the wall to remove her boots. "You've never given me that impression."

"Still." He began unbuttoning her shirt. "A woman needs to feel pursued once in a while. It's good for your self-esteem."

"You're good for my self-esteem."

He threw the shirt aside. Her bra suffered a similar fate. She shivered.

He retrieved the shirt. "That's why I put mine back on." He helped her into it before he finished undressing her.

"You *did* turn the heat up in here."

"I may be crazy about you, but I'm not crazy. I don't want to rush through this because I'm freezing. In a minute or two we won't notice the cold."

It took less than that for Karlea to forget everything except Cody. He did not hurry. They found their way to the sofa. The interlude left them both gasping. She stroked his damp chest.

"I *like* riding the cowboy."

He grinned. "Anytime, ma'am."

She blew in his ear. "What other chores do we need to do today? You've started something I want to continue. In a warmer location."

"I'm plenty warm."

"But you're sweating. I don't want you to catch a chill."

"So are you. I think we're good till evening chores. After a little lunch,

I'm at your disposal all afternoon."

"M-m." She licked her lips. "All afternoon may not do it. We may have to continue this after supper."

He laughed. "The hunter has become the hunted."

Molly began barking and Cody said an expletive.

Karlea climbed off of him. "Oh, no! Someone's here."

Cody grabbed his jeans. "Don't worry. I'll give you some extra time. I can get presentable in a hurry. They'll probably go to the house first."

"Where's my bra?"

"Just button your shirt," he said, tucking his in. "When you put your jacket on, they won't notice."

"Okay."

He pulled a boot on.

"Cody! Karlea!" Kate yelled from the barn door.

"Geez. It *would be* her." He checked that his jeans were over the top of both boots, threw on his jacket, and stepped into the barn aisle. "Hi, Kate. Wasn't expecting you this morning."

"Hi. I need my surcingle. I brought it over when we worked those young horses."

"Sure." He waited for her to reach him.

"Is Karlea out here?"

"Yeah. She's in the tackroom."

"Your shirt's buttoned crooked." He blushed. "Cody, what have you been up to?" She moved closer, began sniffing, then grinned. "You dog."

Cody seized her, pulled her close, and hissed in her ear. "Don't you *dare* tell her that I love her."

He released her, leaving Kate staring. She finally nodded. "O-kay. Step aside."

When they entered the tackroom, Karlea was digging through a box of grooming tools. She smiled. "Good morning, Kate."

"I'll bet it was." She walked to the bridle rack and lifted Karlea's bra from a hook. "Lose something?"

Karlea covered her face. "Oh, my ..."

"I told you you'd like it better than painting his toenails."

Karlea revealed a small smile. "You certainly did. You were certainly right."

"You two are pretty good at keeping secrets."

Cody wrapped his arms around Karlea and leveled his gaze at Kate. "Are you?"

"Don't want this getting around?"

Karlea turned serious. "Please don't tell anyone, Kate. They'll all think Cody's just my boy toy."

Kate laughed. "He's a pretty darned good boy toy. Don't worry. I can keep a secret. And here I thought you were so happy because you moved to Arizona."

"No. I'm happy because Cody came here with me. But I didn't know just how happy I'd be about that."

"Oh, I knew how happy you'd be if he ever treated you to one of his encores. I'll get out of here so he can make his curtain call."

XVIII

As Thanksgiving approached, Cody and Karlea's relationship became more relaxed. She no longer felt desperate to make up for lost time. Sometimes they just took a nap after lunch, without making love.

She planned for her first holiday in her new home, with Deb, her husband, and daughter as guests.

Two days before their arrival, Cody watched the snow fall while drinking his morning coffee. It accumulated on the pickup, but still melted when it hit the ground.

"I never thought of snow in Arizona. I figured the whole state was hot year round."

"And the White Mountains have been covered for a couple weeks already. Do you like it here?"

"Yeah. I guess I'll stay longer than the year I promised you."

"I hoped so. Especially with the new benefit package I've given you."

He smiled and wrapped his arms around her, taking care not to spill his coffee. "Benefits? What benefits?"

"All the nookie you can handle."

"Oh, *those* benefits. They do make coming to work a lot more rewarding. But I'll have to do without them for a few days."

"Darn! And you'll have to sleep in your own bed."

"That's even worse. I like the way you snuggle."

"That's another thing Bill never let me do. Can I ask you something?"

"Sure."

"Did you ever sleep with Deb?"

He laughed so hard that he had to release her. He set his cup on the table. "Heck, no! Deb and I were strictly business."

"Business? You took her to her senior prom."

"Because her boyfriend broke up with her just before. She figured, if she asked any of the guys in her class who were still available, she'd look desperate. But I was out of school and labeled a 'certified hunk' by the senior girls. She made me an offer. I took her on two dates before, and one date after. And I made it look good for her friends. In exchange, she worked with the yearlings three times a week for two months."

Now Karlea laughed. "That explains a lot. I didn't think you and Deb even liked each other. I got very hopeful for that month."

"You wanted us together?"

"I've always thought you were a great guy, Cody."

"Bill didn't. Before that first date he told me to keep it in my pants or he'd cut it off. When Bill Johnson said that, you believed him."

"Oh, my." Her brow furrowed. "I don't think he did that with all her boyfriends."

"He probably thought I wasn't good enough for her. I mean, it's not like she was a vir ..." He stopped with his mouth still open, making Karlea laugh again.

"That isn't news to me. I put her on contraceptives long before her senior prom."

He let his breath out. "Good. Sometimes moms are the last ones to know. And you were right. Deb and I don't like each other. She hasn't liked me since I started working for you. I think she was jealous of the time I spent with you."

"My daughter's like her father that way. Very possessive. She could have spent a lot more time with me if she'd just seen horses as more than a form of transportation. As soon as she could drive, she had no use for them. I still don't know how that happened."

"Why am I horse crazy when no one else in my family is? I didn't get it from my parents. You either have it or you don't."

"Do you think I was a good mom?"

He hugged her again. "You were great. Deb was a little spoiled, but she had rules to follow. She didn't turn out bad."

"So why am I afraid of her? Why can't I tell her that I have a boyfriend and the sex is great?"

He kissed her forehead. "You said she's like Bill. She has his temper. She still doesn't want to share you. She expects you to remain the mourning widow for the rest of your life. And she still doesn't like me. I'll bet she was just thrilled when you told her I was moving here with you."

"She had a fit. Moving was good. But she was sure you couldn't be trusted. She thought you'd take advantage of me."

He smiled. "Do you suppose she was right?"

"I believe sex was my idea."

"See how devious I am? I've convinced you that the whole thing was your idea."

"And I fell for it. I have to go to Basha's and get the rest of my groceries today. But here's another idea. Since we'll have to go without for a few days, shall we spend tomorrow in bed? "

"Sounds good to me. Pick me up a dozen donuts. I've lost some weight."

"Am I working you too hard?"

He grinned. "I'd rather eat more to keep the weight on than give up sex." He refilled his coffee cup. "I noticed that you've never refused me."

"I'm usually the one who starts it. You hardly ever refuse *me*."

"Week after week."

"You make it sound like I should be getting tired of you."

His cheeks reddened. "I've never had a woman who didn't refuse me at least a few days a month."

"Oh-h." She laughed. "Don't worry. That's just one of the many reasons I can't have more kids. My body's so messed up. I might refuse you in another three or four months."

"Really? Like, only once every six months?"

"That's right. Kind of appealing for a young stud."

"Yeah. But kind of selfish too. I know how much you wanted more kids."

"I've gotten over it. I don't have to worry about birth control. And I don't have to refuse my young stud." She licked her lips. "Now, we'd better quit talking about this or I won't get my shopping done."

He grinned. "Yes, ma'am."

***

Deb glared at Cody from the moment she entered the house. Her husband Ted tried to compensate. Cody had liked him from the day they met.

Ted had an even temper, a good quality for dealing with Deb.

Though a city boy, Ted volunteered to help Cody with chores, giving Deb and Karlea time alone.

Deb used the privacy. "Mom, it's totally inappropriate for him to live with you. He needs a place of his own."

Karlea sighed. *I've been expecting this.* "I need him here."

"Don't you care how it looks?"

"No. I suppose I would if he were eighteen. But he's an adult. And so am I."

"You don't care that people think he's screwing you?"

"Deb! Such language! Is that what you think?"

"Of course not. I'm just worried about your reputation."

"I'm a big girl, Deb. My reputation is none of your concern. If I bring home a different man every night, that's my business, not yours. But I'm not living alone. So I'm not lonely and vulnerable. I don't need to bring home strangers."

Deb stared until she recovered her voice. "But you wouldn't do that."

"I tried dating."

"You tried? You've quit?"

"I had a bad experience. Nothing serious. When I decided a retreat was in order, I called Cody. I never doubted he'd come. He didn't hesitate."

"He could still be here for you if he had his own place."

"You're not listening. I need him here. Not miles away. He's right here if I have an emergency."

"You could get him an RV. I noticed lots of places with a house, plus an RV that someone was obviously living in."

"That's true. I *could* do that. But, Deb, I sleep better. Living alone in that house on the ranch, every little sound woke me. I know, if anyone broke in here, they'd have to get past Cody. Don't you want me to feel safe?"

"Of course, I do."

"Ben helped me convince Cody to move here. Ben trusts him. Why can't you?"

Deb scowled. "I guess if Ben trusts him, I can too."

"You should be able to trust him based on your own experience. He's worked for me for almost ten years. What's he ever done to earn your animosity?"

"He's always been so smug. He shares your love of horses and I don't."

Karlea shook her head. She had never seen a shred of smugness from Cody. "Why don't you just admit that you're jealous?"

"Okay! I am!"

"Well, then this is your problem, not mine or Cody's. I'm happy here. I want you to be happy for me too. If you can't be, I'm not going to lose any sleep over it."

Deb stared.

Karlea felt warm inside. *I've always placated her. She needed to hear me tell it like it is for a change. Guess I shocked her.*

Finally, Deb nodded. "I still don't like him, but I'll try to be nicer. He seems to be taking pretty good care of you."

"He's so good to me. Last week when I didn't feel good, he did all the chores, inside and out. He even brought me something to eat when I felt up to it."

"You let him in *your bedroom*?"

"It would be tough to have breakfast in bed any other way. He couldn't stand in the doorway and throw it at me."

Deb laughed. "That's exactly how I want it served next time. A bottle of juice and a bagel should be easy to throw. Oh, Darla's awake. That trip really wore her out."

***

"I want you so much," Karlea said, between kisses.

Cody pushed his hands under her jacket, knowing they did not have time to make love. Even if they had the time, he had not thought to turn up the heat in the tackroom. A temperature below fifty degrees did not lend itself to a romantic liaison under any circumstances.

And they needed to finish chores before they returned to the house for supper. Deb had decided to cook this evening.

"When they leave," he promised. "I'm keeping you in bed all day." He kissed her neck. "We'll have to settle for a taste now."

"Are you sure we can't make love? You're pretty creative."

"We might have to be pretty creative when we get to the house too."

"Oh. You think they'd notice?"

"Possible."

"Okay. Just a taste then."

In the middle of their next kiss, the door opened and Ted froze in mid-stride. Karlea gripped Cody and tears came.

He kissed her forehead. "Don't worry. He doesn't want to be the one to tell her about this. Do you, Ted?"

"God, no! I don't want to be within a hundred miles when *you* tell her."

"There. Nothing to worry about."

Karlea wiped her eyes. "Thanks, Ted."

"Don't thank me. Forget I was here. Especially when you tell Deb. When do you plan to tell her?"

"I don't. It's not like we're getting married. We're just having fun."

Ted fought hard not to smile, but finally surrendered. "Good for you."

"And before you ask, he didn't seduce me. It was my idea."

"I wasn't planning to ask, but she wears off on me. The thought crossed my mind. So Cody, you like working for Karlea?"

"I finally get to brag about this. She offers great fringe benefits."

They laughed, but she blushed. "I guess you've been holding that in. Ted, Deb isn't the only one we're keeping in the dark. Nobody knows about this."

"They won't hear it from me."

"Why'd you come out here anyhow? We thought you were helping Deb."

"She sent me out here to ask you something. What was it?" He snapped his fingers. "Oh, yeah. She can't find your pie plates."

"In the cupboard around the corner from the fridge."

"Okay. I'll leave you to your 'chores' then." He made quotation marks with his fingers.

XIX

When Karlea's guests left the yard, Cody locked the door. Clothes came off within two minutes and he carried her to the bedroom, feeling his way while kissing her. He put her down, then fell back on the bed, allowing her to come to him.

She smiled. "Very thoughtful, letting me control the pace."

"After four days, I might rush through this."

She hovered over him, deliciously close. "I could tease you indefinitely from this vantage point."

He pushed himself to a half-seated position, bringing his lips to within inches of hers. "I'll bet I can bring you to me with nothing but my mouth."

Her breath quickened. "Show me."

He began delivering wet kisses. When he required contortions to reach his targets, she moved to accommodate him. He accomplished his goal in short order. After very intense love making, she lay on him and sighed.

"You have a very talented mouth."

"I know how to get what I want. That's the first time you've played hard to get. You could do that once in awhile."

"A nice change from my randy grandmother routine?"

He let his hands slide across her body. "I don't see a grandmother. I see a very hot woman. That little doll who looks just like you is an illusion. You're far too young to be a grandmother."

"You silver-tongued devil. You already have my body. Is there some special sexual favor you wanted?"

"I don't need flattery to get it. I know you'd give me anything I asked for." She blushed. "Because I'd never ask too much."

"I trust you not to ask for anything bizarre. You've made sex interesting."

"Interesting, huh? Glad I'm not boring you."

"Not even close. I managed to get through Deb's visit without lying to her."

"Must have taken some doing. For the first time in my life, I'm not looking forward to Christmas."

"I know! We'll be apart for eight days. Why did we ever agree to that?"

"When I planned this trip, I wasn't satisfying your every desire. Can't tell Mom and Dad that I have to get back here because Karlea's hot to trot."

"Uff da! No. You're flying from Phoenix. How'd you like to spend a romantic night there when you come back?"

"You talked me into it. We don't even have to spend the whole time in bed. I'd enjoy going out as a couple instead of employer and employee."

"Oh-h. Would you take me dancing?"

"Sure. Having something to look forward to will make the time apart easier."

"Here's an even better idea. Two romantic nights. I'll just tell Hank and Kate that you're not coming in for another day."

"Karlea, that's a bald-faced lie."

"I know. If I were more like Dotty, I'd tell the world that I'm bedding a twenty-four-year-old and enjoying it very much, thank you. But since I'm not, we have to sneak around. I look forward to a public show of affection."

Cody rubbed her back and tried to muster the nerve to confess his love. "I'd like that too."

"It's a date, then."

"I like the sound of that."

"What's wrong?"

He swallowed. "What could be wrong? I have a naked woman draped over me."

"Don't be glib. I've known you too long. Something's bothering you."

Tell her! Don't be a coward! "Just those guilty feelings again."

"I'm sorry. I feel them too. If they get too bad, you can stop this."

He sighed. "If they get too bad, I work them off in bed. How's the song go? 'I'm old enough to know better, but still too young to care'."

"Could that apply to me too? At times I really get down on myself. Then you flash that smile and I quit thinking. We both think what we're doing is wrong, don't we?"

"Yeah. I guess I want you more than I want a clear conscience."

"Um-m."

He changed the subject, afraid to think about it too much. "By the way, what did you say to Deb? She was almost *nice* to me."

"We had a long talk. I got her to admit that she's jealous. Then she could finally open her eyes to how good you treat me. She made a lot of progress the past few days."

"Must have. I actually enjoyed their visit."

"Darla fell in love with you."

"I'm good with kids."

"Yes, you are. I'm wasting your time. You should be looking for a woman who can give you children."

He tilted her chin up and kissed her softly. "Don't worry about me. I have plenty of time for that. I'll let you know if I feel my biological clock ticking. But I can ignore that too. If I find a woman who can give me children, I'll have to use condoms again. And I *like* this unsafe sex."

"You can be such a *man*."

"Thanks."

"That wasn't a compliment."

***

As Karlea and Cody kissed, she hoped desperately that only strangers frequented the Phoenix airport this day. She finally broke away to speak.

"I've missed you so much."

"I noticed. I've missed you too. Let's get out of here." He wrapped his arm around her while they walked through the terminal.

"I've missed more than your body."

"Me too. Although, at the moment, your body is most on my mind."

She slid her hand into his back pocket. "Let's not talk about that till we get to the hotel. We'll drive ourselves crazy. How were your folks?"

They managed to keep themselves occupied until they reached the hotel. But they abandoned conversation in the elevator, turning a few heads with their long kisses.

After they made love, Cody hugged her and sighed. "I hate leaving you. I wish I could say that to people who think I should be glad to get away for a while."

"I know. I'm sorry it has to be this way."

"I knew it going in. I could have said no."

"We discussed that before. I know you couldn't refuse me."

"I could have. You didn't coerce me. I just prefer not to refuse you. I like seeing you happy."

"Oh, I am." She kissed his chest. "And what you do to me feels more loving than anything Bill ever did."

"Maybe it is."

She met his gaze. "What do you mean?"

Just say it, Cody. Tell her how you feel. "I treasure you. Did you ever feel like he treasured you?"

"No. I don't remember anything he did that made me feel loved, or even treasured. I felt needed. It was good enough at the time. When the boys grew up, I didn't even feel that. Being treasured is so much better."

"Good." *Coward!*

He kissed her softly and slid his hand down her body, stopping on her belly. The expected amorous response failed to materialize. Instead, she removed his hand.

She offered a self-conscious apology. "I'm sorry. I porked out so much over the holidays, I'm embarrassed. I need to go on a diet when we get home."

"You think you're getting fat?"

"I *know* I'm getting fat. I only have one pair of jeans I can sit down in."

"Really? I didn't notice."

"You're so sweet."

"Well, you're not the only one who gained weight. I must have put on five pounds while I was home."

"You needed it. Did your mom ask if I was feeding you?"

"She noticed. I told her you're wearing me out with sex."

"Sure, you did. How can you lose weight on twice a day sex while I gain?"

"It's more work for me."

"Usually."

"And self-preservation."

"Huh?"

"Lower metabolism. Women will still be going strong long after men starve to death."

She chuckled. "I see. I'd better rev up my exercise program."

He licked his lips. "Be glad to help you with that."

"I don't want to kill you just so I can lose weight."

"You thought I was talking about sex? I plan to wake you at five AM and send you out jogging."

She hit him. "You're *so* thoughtful."

"Just the kind of guy I am."

***

Karlea stepped up her exercise program. She had already been riding most days, using the indoor arena during inclement weather. She added walking and even cross-country skied for several days after a substantial snow. She could not remove the "fat food" from the house. Cody needed it. Instead, she practiced strict portion control, measuring everything before it entered her mouth.

Cody's level of support surprised her. He provided words of encouragement when she most needed them.

Preparing for bed one evening, she sighed as she studied her naked body in a full-length mirror. He hugged and kissed her.

"What's wrong, beautiful?"

She smiled, but began crying. "Thank you. I haven't gained any more. But it's discouraging when I don't lose."

"You've just reached a plateau. It happens to everyone. Muscle weighs more than fat and look at the muscle you've built."

"What makes you an expert? You've never had to worry about your weight."

"Listening to Mom. She's tried everything."

"Sure. I remember we were in the same weight loss group after Deb was born." Her smile faded and more tears came.

"What's wrong?"

"He called me a fat pig. He told me that I really let myself go."

"Who? When?"

"Bill. After Deb was born. I had trouble taking off the weight. Everything was so new. I didn't have time to eat right."

"He was an insensitive jerk. There's no excuse for being cruel to the person you love."

"Maybe he didn't love me, Cody. I'm having more doubts about that every day."

He kissed her forehead. "You can't change the past. You have me now and I love you more than he ever did." *There! I said it! Finally!*

She sighed and nodded. "Oh, thank you. You're right. I have a lot of friends who love me more than he did. I should appreciate you rather than dwell on the past."

He hugged her, biting his lip. *Do I have to draw her a picture? I finally tell her that I love her and she doesn't get it. Will she ever be able to think of me like a husband?* "Let's go to bed."

He just held her until she fell asleep. Then he sighed. He suddenly felt trapped by his own choices.

It took me four years to tell her that I love her. And I can't say "no" to her, no matter how guilty I feel. No wonder she takes me for granted. I'm not just her boy toy. I'm her right hand man. That makes me indispensable.

He let out a ragged breath. *But it can't make her love me. Maybe I need to end this.* At least he would have a clear conscience. She had told him at the start that he could do that. If he ended it, she would expect an explanation. *Then I could tell her that I love her too much for a casual affair.*

That won't work. Not when she's struggling with her weight. She'll just think I'm not attracted to her anymore because she's gotten too fat. I'd better just leave things as they are till she has her weight under control.

XX

After two months of dieting and exercise, Karlea had gained another five pounds. When discouragement became concern, she made an appointment to see a doctor in Show Low. Not wanting Cody to worry, she told him that she had errands to run.

She filled out volumes of forms before a nurse led her to an exam room and began gathering information. Karlea explained her concern.

"Do you diet frequently?"

"No. I only had problems with my weight once, when I was pregnant."

"Any chance of that?"

Karlea laughed. "None."

"When was your last menstrual period?"

"Don't read anything into this. September. About twice a year is all I can manage. One of the many reasons why I can't have children."

"Have you been sexually active?"

Karlea blushed. "Yes."

"Are you using contraceptives?"

"What's the point? I'm not pregnant."

"I'll check with the doctor. He'll probably want to do a pregnancy test, just to rule it out."

"If it will make him feel better."

Karlea chuckled to herself. The nurse had no idea how emphatic her family doctor had been. Even with modern fertility techniques, he had assured her that she had no chance of having another baby.

The nurse returned with the test, explained to an inexperienced Karlea how to use it, then left her alone.

She stared at the results. Finally, she forced her feet to move, taking it to the nurse. "This is *wrong*."

"The doctor ordered some lab work if you got a positive. Come with me."

"It's not possible."

"The test's very accurate, ma'am."

"It's never wrong?"

"Ninety-nine percent."

"I'm the one percent."

After her lab work, Karlea saw the doctor. He glanced at her chart. "Sue tells me that you dispute the pregnancy test results."

"With good reason. I was told that I could never have another baby. I begged my doctor to give me some hope. He refused. He said there were far too many things wrong with me."

"I try not to tell a woman she'll never have a baby unless she's had a hysterectomy. An ultrasound will settle this. I checked. They can get you in at two-thirty. Drink a lot of water before the exam."

"I feel like I'm wasting my time and yours."

"Mrs. Johnson, you have unexplained weight gain and a positive pregnancy test. Despite your history, I will assume pregnancy until I see proof to the contrary."

"Okay."

She walked outside to use her cell phone. "Dotty, are you busy?"

"What do you need?"

"I'm at the clinic in Show Low. I'm having an ultrasound at 2:30. I could use some moral support."

"I'll be there."

***

When Dotty arrived, Karlea told her what little she knew. Dotty held her hand and accompanied her to the exam.

The female technician placed a transducer on Karlea's lower abdomen and watched the monitor. Almost immediately, she spoke cheerfully. "There's your baby."

"No!"

Karlea's tears startled the woman. Dotty comforted her friend while the exam continued. Even their untrained eyes could identify a very active baby.

Dotty asked questions. "How far along is she?"

"The doctor will tell you for certain. But the measurements look like about twenty weeks."

"Can you tell if it's a boy or a girl?"

"Too early for me. Mrs. Johnson, we're done here. Your doctor wants you back at the clinic."

Dotty led her to the dressing room and coached her through the most basic tasks. Karlea followed her to the clinic, still crying. Seeing her state, Sue ushered them to the doctor's office. During the twenty minutes they waited there, Karlea's tears never subsided.

When the doctor entered, he studied her. "Mrs. Johnson, it's good that you have a supportive friend. Will your baby's father also be supportive?"

Dotty waited for her to reply, then answered the question. "He's always taken good care of her. I can't imagine that would change."

"Good. She needs a lot of support through this initial shock."

"No," Karlea said. "I can't tell him."

Dotty gaped. "He has to know."

"No."

"Why?"

"I told him we were just having fun. I told him we didn't need to use protection. I was so *stupid*!"

"Mrs. Johnson, will you see this man again?"

"Yes."

"Then you have no choice but to tell him. You are twenty-two weeks along. He's bound to notice." She cried harder. "Would you like something to help you relax?"

She shrugged. The doctor phoned his nurse to order an injection.

Dotty felt protective. "Is that safe for the baby?"

"Safe and very mild. It will relieve her anxiety. I wish that physicians wouldn't tell women that they can't have children. We see supposedly barren, pregnant women on a regular basis. It's always a shock."

"Karlea had fifteen years of marriage as proof that he was right. How do you explain that?"

"I see. More than the usual shock. The father of this baby isn't the same man she was married to for those years?"

"No."

"We'll have a look at her medical records." Sue entered and gave Karlea the injection. "Sue, did you have Mrs. Johnson sign a release for her medical records?"

"Yes, doctor."

"We'll send for those right away." He scanned papers in Karlea's clinic chart. "Frankly, the tests we ran were all within normal parameters. Right now, I see no reason why she couldn't have more children. Mrs. Johnson, are you feeling a little better?"

"A little."

"Good. You are twenty-two weeks along and your baby seems fine. All your lab work is normal. I see no reason why you can't carry this baby to term. Have you had other children?"

"One. She's twenty."

"While that's a long time between pregnancies, you're healthy and in good physical condition. It shouldn't be a problem. Do you remember when you were told that you couldn't have more children?"

"On Deb's second birthday."

"That will save me some time when I look through your medical records. I want to see you in two weeks, just to re-evaluate your emotional state. Do you have any questions?"

"Are you sure this isn't a horrible mistake?"

"I'm very sure that you're pregnant. It's all a matter of your attitude whether you consider it a mistake or not."

Dotty walked her to the parking lot. "Do you need anything from your car? I'll drive you home."

"I can't go home! I can't face him."

"Okay. I'll take you to my place for now. I'll make excuses for you."

"Thank you, Dotty. What would I do without you?"

***

Dotty called Cody. He did not give her a chance to speak.

"Dotty, have you seen Karlea?"

"She's with me."

"Thank God. I've been trying to call her. Did she turn off her cell phone?"

"Yeah. She has something to work through. She's staying with me tonight."

"With you? Why can't she come home? Did I do something wrong?"

"No, Cody. She just needs another woman to talk to."

"O-kay. Tell her I miss her. If she needs me, I'll be here."

"I will." She disconnected. "Cody misses you."

"He's so sweet. I'm so ashamed of myself. I took advantage of his loyalty, then I didn't have sense enough to use protection. He *offered* to use protection."

"Karlea, you had unprotected sex for fifteen years. Why would you start now?"

"I should have."

"You can't change the past. Quit putting yourself down. You're going to have the baby you always wanted."

"I wanted Bill's baby. My husband's baby."

"Cody will be a better father than Bill ever was."

"How does this look? I seduced a young man to get this baby. I can already hear the snickers."

"It's time you did what's right for you instead of worrying about what other people think. Quit feeling sorry for yourself."

"How do I tell Deb that she's about to become a big sister? She'll hate me!"

Dotty shook her head. "One problem at a time. You don't have to worry about that for at least a couple months. You have to tell Cody tomorrow."

"I can't."

"I'll help you."

"Oh, thank you, Dotty!"

XXI

Karlea slept for twelve hours, then managed to remain tear-free through breakfast. Dotty asked her three times when she wanted to go home, getting no reply. Dotty finally announced that they were leaving. Karlea just nodded. She said nothing during the drive.

When Dotty pulled into the yard, Cody hurried from the barn. Karlea saw him and began sobbing.

He opened the car door and hugged her. "What's wrong? Please let me help you."

"You're so sweet."

She unbuckled her seatbelt, then let him help her out of the car. But she pulled away and shuffled toward the house. He looked from her to Dotty, then caught up to her.

He remained silent until she had perched on the edge of her favorite chair. "What's wrong, Dotty? Why won't she tell me?"

Dotty sat on the arm of Karlea's chair rubbing her back. He began pacing.

"She's just had a shock," Dotty said.

"Did someone die?"

"No. Karlea, do you want me to tell him?"

"No."

"If I don't tell him, you have to."

Karlea sighed. "Go ahead."

"She saw a doctor about the weight she's gained."

"Is something wrong with her?"

"No-o. There's no easy way to say this. She's pregnant."

He froze. *I heard her wrong. That's impossible.* No. Dotty had said "pregnant." The room began to move and he reached for the nearest chair, slumping into it. He leaned forward and covered his face to fight the dizziness.

Pregnant. She can't be pregnant. He raised his head. "But ..."

"That's what we said. Her doctor in North Dakota said she couldn't get pregnant. He was wrong."

He hid his face again, struggling to think. *I gave Karlea the baby she always wanted. She's just in shock. When she gets over that, she'll be happy. She'll love me for it. She was probably afraid that I'd be angry. I need to tell her I'm not.* He raised his head.

"Wow. That sure is a shock. But, wow. A baby. I kind of like the idea."

Dotty smiled, but he saw disbelief in Karlea's face.

"You're proud of this?"

"I wouldn't say proud. But you said I should be a father."

"Not of *my* baby!"

Cody sat up straight and bit his lip. He hesitated. "But you wanted more children."

"Sure! Ten years ago! When I was married."

"You don't want this baby?"

"It doesn't matter what I want. I can't change it."

"It matters *to me.*"

"This baby just means everyone will know that I've been bedding a twenty-four-year-old."

Cody fought tears. *I won't let her see me cry! She's that ashamed of me. I'm such a fool. She'll never fall in love with me. I'm just her stable hand.*

He ran his hands through his hair. "Well, I guess I know where I stand. I'm getting out of here."

"You're leaving?"

"Oh, don't worry. I don't walk out on a job. I'll come do your chores till I decide what to do. But I'm getting away from *you!*" He stalked to his room and slammed the door.

She sighed. "I knew he'd be angry."

Dotty shook her head. Karlea had managed to hurt Cody into anger, yet had no clue. "I'll talk to him."

She knocked on Cody's door and entered without waiting for a reply. He stopped jamming clothes into an overnight bag and turned his back to her. He wiped his eyes. "Don't try to change my mind!"

"She's confused, Cody."

"She sounded loud and clear to me! She doesn't want *my* baby! I'm good enough to do her chores and satisfy all her fantasies, but ... I'm not ... good enough to be ... the father of her baby." He wiped his eyes again.

"That's not what she meant."

"Well, then she has a real problem with the English language. That's what she said."

She rubbed his back, realizing that now two people could not think clearly. She placed a key in his hand. "Stay in my guest house. It's free and you'll be close."

After a moment, he sighed. "On one condition. I don't want to see her. I need time to think. Don't let her come."

"Okay. You can see her when you're ready to talk."

"Yeah. Right."

***

Dotty stayed with Karlea all day. She only ate when prodded. At bedtime, she stood by her bed crying before returning to the livingroom to lay on the sofa. Dotty spent the night, only leaving the next morning after feeding Karlea again.

True to his word, Cody had done chores in the evening and morning. He returned to Dotty's guest house to find she had left food for him. He had only eaten the non-perishable snack foods in the cupboards. In his state of mind, even facing strangers seemed too much to endure. He ate with gratitude.

He sank into a chair and kicked off his boots. Molly lay her head on his knee and he absentmindedly stroked her. Twenty-four hours had failed to dull the pain. He drew a ragged breath and silently berated himself.

Quit acting like a victim. You volunteered to let her trample on you. You didn't want an affair, but did you say that? No. You went along with her because you were too scared to say, "I love you." You ignored your conscience. You reacted out of fear. You were afraid she'd find someone else.

Tears came.

Look what it got you. You deserve this. You thought you'd win her love by sleeping with her. Well, guess what. If she didn't fall in love with you after everything you've done for her, that wasn't going to do it.

"I want to go home."

Molly thumped her tail and he wiped his eyes. He would get away from Karlea and the hurt by returning to his home and family.

"My family? I can't leave my baby."

She may not want my baby, but I do. I'll take it. I'll tell her that. If she just has it, I'll take it off her hands. Then I'll go home. Is it a boy or a girl? I don't care. I love it no matter what.

Planning for his first child should have been a happy occasion. Karlea had ruined it for him. Again he scolded himself for forgetting that he shared some of the responsibility.

He did not care what anyone thought. *Anyone except Karlea.* He felt ashamed of what he had done. But he would not be ashamed of his child. *Like she is.*

***

After three days, Cody needed more clothes. He finished morning chores and stood by the pickup for some time before carrying his overnight bag to the front door. He knocked and entered.

Karlea sat up on the sofa. Her hair looked as if it had not been combed or washed since he left. She wore her robe and seemed to have taken up residence in the livingroom. Beverage containers and tissues lay scattered about the floor. Little light penetrated the drapes. She appeared pale and sickly.

Cody stared, then let Molly in. She went to Karlea, who hugged her. He said only what he needed to.

"Just came for clothes."

He strode to his room and stuffed clothes into the bag. When he returned, Karlea looked up from petting Molly.

"I'm sorry I hurt you."

He stared at the door for a moment before facing her. "That's good. But how would you introduce me to someone? As your horse trainer? Or as the father of your baby?" She dropped her gaze. "That's what I thought! Well, here's my offer! I want this baby. So after you have it, we'll both be out of your life. You can pretend it never happened. That should make you happy! Come, Molly."

Molly hesitated as Karlea began crying. "Please, let her stay."

His anger melted. "Don't forget to let her out."

He stalked to the pickup, started it, but waited a moment before shifting into gear. "Why are you being such a jerk?"

He knew that he was striking back for the way she had hurt him. But the momentary relief gave way to guilt. He wanted nothing more than to help her through this difficult time. But she had rejected him. Cody had never felt worse in his life.

He eased the pickup out of the yard.

XXII

Cody found Molly outside when he did chores the next morning. He entered the house before leaving, on the pretense of putting her in. Karlea looked up from the sofa.

"Just letting Molly in."

Later, Dotty stopped by to make lunch for Karlea. She had been unable to talk her friend out of her depression. But at least she could make sure that she ate.

When someone rang the bell, she hoped to see Cody. Instead, her brother stood at the front door.

"It's Hank."

"Tell him to go away."

"No." Dotty opened the door. "Morning, Hank."

"What the heck's going on?"

"Come in."

"Cody's pickup's been at your guest house most of the week and you're over here." He saw Karlea. "Good God, what happened to you?" He took a chair facing her.

She looked up at him. "I'm getting what I deserve."

"What? Explain."

"I'm pregnant."

He opened his mouth several times before the words exploded. "That S O B!"

"No, Hank. If you want to swear at someone, swear at me. Cody has never refused me and I took advantage of that. It was my idea."

He rubbed his chin, then stared at his hands before looking at her again. "Okay. So you're getting the baby you always wanted and he feels like you trapped him."

"No. He wants the baby. I don't."

"You don't! How many years did we listen to you wish for a baby? You would've adopted if Bill had let you. Why aren't you jumping for joy?"

"Because everyone will know that I seduced a twenty-four-year-old to get it."

"Well, isn't that *too bad!* Quit feeling sorry for yourself! Your prayer is answered, but not in the perfect way you had in mind. Cody pulled off a miracle for you and all you can think about is *your reputation.*"

A single tear rolled down her cheek. "You could be right."

"Better believe it. That boy would walk through fire for you. He'd be here, but I'm guessing you punched him in the gut. You would've had to hurt him bad to make him run off."

She nodded. "I've treated him like I'm ashamed of him. I'm ashamed of myself, not him. He deserves better."

"Yeah, he does. You owe him one heck of an apology."

"But he's avoiding me."

"I'll have a talk with him."

***

Hank did not drive directly to Dotty's farm. He needed to deal with his jealousy. Karlea had no interest in him. But she had pursued Cody, apparently not for love, just for fun. He would have gladly given her a fling. She only had to ask.

He finally accepted her decision and parked by the guest house. Cody did not answer his knock, so he opened the door. Cody's eyes widened, then he stiffened.

Hank tried to put him at ease. "So she broke your heart too."

Cody's shoulders settled back in his chair. "Yeah."

"Women! Can't live with 'em. Can't live without 'em."

He sat and Cody nodded.

"Now I understand what that means."

"The first broken heart is the worst. What did she say that hurt so much?"

Cody covered his face for a moment. He lowered his hands. "I'm not good enough for her. She's ashamed to tell people that I'm the father of her baby."

"Were those her exact words?"

"No. She said she didn't want me to be the father of her baby. I got the message."

"I think you got the wrong one. Want to know what she meant?"

Cody hesitated. "I'm pretty sure I know what she meant."

"You're wrong. She'd just gotten the biggest shock of her life. She's still not making much sense. Do you suppose she was in top form when you talked to her?"

"Well, no."

"Then, listen. She was trying to tell you that she's ashamed of herself."

"Herself? That's not how it came out."

"She feels like she took advantage of your loyalty. Now everyone will know. She feels humiliated by what *she did*. Not because of who you are."

"She's not ashamed of me?"

"Not a bit. And she knows her words came out wrong when you talked. She feels even worse about that." He gave Cody time to think about it.

"She didn't take advantage of me. I'm an adult. I had choices."

"True. What was your first reaction when she propositioned you?"

"I didn't want that." He sighed. "I love her."

"I thought so."

"Don't tell her."

"That's your job. She's probably not ready to hear that."

"That's the problem. The timing's never right. If I say it now, she'll think I'm just being noble. If I had any guts, I would've told her years ago."

"Years?"

"Since I was twenty. Pretty pathetic that I couldn't get up the courage to tell her once in four years."

"Don't be so hard on yourself. Bill was alive for part of that time. It would've been dumb to say it then. Afterward, I'm sure you wanted to wait a respectful time before saying it."

"Yeah."

"And she said she used to babysit you."

"Used to remind me of that all the time."

"It's not like falling in love with a classmate. Everything's changed between you two. You hung in there till she could see you as her partner instead of a kid. You stuck with it till she could even see you as a lover. Just hang in there a little longer. You need to go home."

Cody nodded. "Thanks. You made that possible. I'm worried about her. But I couldn't go thinking she had no respect for me."

"That's what friends are for. How long have you two been sharing a bed?"

"October 11th."

"Just wondered, with all her fertility problems, how long you had to work to make that baby. You're pretty good. Dotty said she's twenty-two weeks."

Cody made some calculations in the air. "That's five months! That was almost right away. How could that happen?"

"Your daddy should have explained that to you. But knowing that S O B she was married to, he was probably shooting blanks. Just convinced her that it was her problem."

"I didn't like him either. But a doctor gave her the news."

"It was a small town. Could the doctor have been one of Bill's buddies?"

"He *was*. They went hunting and fishing all the time."

"Makes sense to me."

XXIII

Cody took time to prepare himself. Karlea might still say hurtful things until she adjusted to her condition. He needed to toughen up in order to help her.

He thought about his baby. *I'll be a father in four months, the father of Karlea's baby.* He had hoped to some day be her husband. But loving her had meant letting go of ever becoming a father. Hank had told him to hang in there. *Maybe, if I'm patient, she'll fall in love with me yet.*

His chest felt tight. That dream seemed too far out of reach. Better to just forget that one for now. His love had given her the baby she wanted. It might take time. *But I know she'll be happy about it after awhile. After she gets over feeling ashamed.*

He thanked a very relieved Dotty and drove home. He entered the house without knocking. Karlea looked up.

"Can I come home?"

She nodded and ran to him, sobbing. "I'm so sorry, Cody."

"I know. I'm sorry too. I was hurting and I said some mean things."

"I'm sorry I hurt you. I just feel so ashamed. But when I opened my mouth, everything came out wrong."

"I know that now." He squeezed her. "You need to take better care of yourself. Right now you're going to take a shower, wash your hair, brush your teeth, and put on clean clothes."

"Okay."

After she departed, he opened the drapes and began cleaning the livingroom. He finished that and checked the kitchen. Dotty had kept that clean. He put together a casserole for supper. It could cook while he did chores.

Karlea rejoined him, almost looking like herself again. He hugged her.

"Much better. When's your next doctor visit?"

"I don't know. I think Dotty wrote it on the calender."

He checked. "The end of next week. I'm going with you. Before long, people will notice that you're pregnant. There's no point in trying to keep me a secret any longer."

She sat by the kitchen table, then nodded. "Okay."

"I have so much to learn about babies and pregnancy. I'll ask a lot of questions. I want to enjoy this."

"Enjoy it? It just doesn't seem real yet. I keep hoping this is a nightmare and I'll wake up."

He kissed her forehead. "It'll get better. Once you get over the shock, you'll be happy."

"Will I?"

"You've wanted a baby for so long. I really believe you'll be happy. But maybe not until you see our baby."

"Maybe when I hold it?"

"Yeah."

"Maybe."

***

Cody had to urge Karlea to eat. After clearing the table, he sent her to bed early, then retired himself. He undressed, feeling exhausted.

Karlea opened his door, tears in her eyes. "Aren't you going to sleep with me?"

"No. I can't do that anymore. It hurts too much."

"I can't sleep alone."

"Yes, you can."

"No. I haven't been sleeping without you."

"I won't do that."

"Not sex. Just let me snuggle with you."

"Karlea, you're just making this harder for both of us."

"I'm sorry. Just two nights. Please. I'll be better."

He sighed. "Okay. But just two nights. Go to bed. I'll be right there."

He pulled on a pair of sweat pants and shuffled to her bedroom. His emotions threatened to spill over as she melted into his arms. She slept almost immediately, while he lay awake, fighting tears.

I still can't say "no" to her. No more sleeping together. That conviction lasted a long time. How long before she talks me into sex?

He sighed and wiped his eyes. *I won't give in. I'm tired of volunteering to feel guilty and hurt.*

***

Karlea improved. She slept alone the third night, but only after telling Cody that he could choose to stay. She began making her own decisions and performing household chores. She still spoke very little and sometimes began crying for no apparent reason. He hugged her often.

The day of her appointment, she tried to convince him to stay home. He refused. He struggled with hurt feelings when she kept a chair between them in the waiting room. *Remember, she's feeling ashamed of herself, not you.*

Once they moved to the doctor's office, she allowed him to hold her hand. The doctor entered and introduced himself to Cody. He studied Karlea's chart.

"Mrs. Johnson, how are you feeling today?"

"Better. I've accepted my punishment."

The doctor raised his eyes, then looked from Karlea to Cody, who shrugged. He asked another question.

"Why do you feel you're being punished?"

"I thought I'd have a secret affair, go a little wild. No one would ever know. I forgot that God knows. He's punishing me."

"Is that how you see it, Mr. Pfeiffer?"

"No. Sure, we *both* deserved to have our affair exposed. But for as long as I can remember, Karlea's talked about the baby she couldn't have. I can't look at this baby as punishment. I think of it as the answer to her prayers."

"Mrs. Johnson, what do you think of that perspective?"

"When I was married, I prayed for a baby. When Bill died, I gave up that dream. The people close to me all want this baby for me. They think I should be happy about it."

"No one can tell you what to feel. I think the joy will come eventually. You'll realize that you gave up your dream too soon. For now, you're dwelling on the negative consequences of your pregnancy. There are positive consequences as well."

"There are? Maybe. I'll try to remind myself of that."

"Good. Your medical records arrived rather quickly. After reviewing them, I tried to call this Dr. Smith and learned that he had passed away."

"About a year ago."

"That will save him a malpractice lawsuit. I found nothing in your test results to indicate infertility."

"Nothing! But he told me that everything was out of wack."

"The only thing 'out of wack', as you put it, is your menstrual cycle. That has little to do with fertility." He put on his glasses. "Even more troubling. Quoting from the physician's notes. 'Discussed fertility test results with Mrs. Johnson and her husband.' End quote."

"He didn't mention what he said to me?"

"For good reason. No evidence of malpractice. It would be your word against his."

"But Bill was there."

Cody gripped the arm of his chair. "If there's nothing wrong with her, why didn't she get pregnant? There had to be something wrong with Bill."

"Perhaps. I hate to even suggest this, but your medical records raise the question of ethics violations. Were Dr. Smith and your husband friends?"

"Best friends. Hunting and fishing buddies."

Cody's knuckles turned white. "He wasn't man enough to admit he had a problem! He lied to her. He made her think she had a problem when he knew how much she wanted another baby."

"It's just a theory, Mr. Pfeiffer."

"You didn't know that ... him. It's a good theory. It's the kind of thing he would have done."

Karlea's lip trembled. She nodded. "I'm afraid Cody's right. I was naive. I'm starting to see that I was married to a very selfish man."

"Mrs. Johnson, if you will sign a release for your late husband's medical records, I'll investigate further."

"Of course."

"Very good. Now, I'll prescribe pre-natal vitamins and schedule routine obstetric check-ups. Of course, no alcohol. Other than that, I have no special instructions. Continue your usual activities. You are in fine condition to carry a baby. Any questions?"

Cody answered. "About a hundred."

The doctor laughed. "I'll give you some literature. But I have time for a few questions."

"Is it okay for her to keep riding?"

"Horses, I assume. She can continue anything she has been doing. But don't take unnecessary risks. Don't ride bucking horses or jump fences."

Karlea frowned. "Not even little fences?"

"Does it increase your risk of a fall?"

"I suppose."

"Then don't."

"She won't. She's been dieting, walking, and cross-country skiing."

"Quit dieting. Continue the other. Since you're a first time father, I'll anticipate another question. Continue sexual activity as before. For now."

Cody dropped his eyes. "No, doctor. Then we would have learned nothing from all this."

"That's your choice. If any questions remain after you read the literature, you can ask them on your next visit."

"Thanks."

Karlea did not release Cody's hand when they left the office, walked through the waiting room, or crossed the parking lot.

He stopped by the pickup and looked into her eyes. "You finally seem at peace. What's changed?"

"Maybe just my attitude. But you helped change it. You got so angry when you realized what Bill did to me. I did a better job picking the father of this baby than I did the first one." His lip quivered and he hugged her very hard. "I'm so sorry for how I hurt you."

"It's okay. That's behind us. Neither of us were prepared for a baby."

"In any way. Please, take me to K-mart. These sweat pants just aren't cutting it. I need maternity clothes."

"Yes, ma'am."

"Don't say that. It makes me feel old."

XXIV

"Have you thought about names?" Cody asked three weeks later.

"Not seriously. Do you know why your parents picked your name?"

"We'd better sit down for that story."

"It's that complicated?"

"Complicated, and not all that pleasant."

She took his hand and they sat on the sofa. "Go on."

"The simple answer—the one my parents tell people—is that they took a romantic trip to Cody, Wyoming about the time I was conceived. The truth is, they went there not long after I was conceived. Mom needed some time to learn to trust Dad again."

She gasped. "Did he cheat on her?"

"No. Never. She didn't trust any man, not even the one she loved. Mom was raped."

"Oh, my. I didn't know."

"Neither does anyone else. They've never told anyone but me."

"Why would they tell you?"

"Because it happened nine months before I was born."

Karlea stared, slack jawed. She realized it and closed her mouth. "Everyone said you were a miracle. After they adopted five kids. But Allen isn't your father."

"Yes, he is. He's my dad and my father. That rapist isn't my father. And, if I ever find out who he is, I'll punch him in the mouth. But Mom and Dad turned that terrible experience around and managed to feel grateful for me. Mom wanted to have a baby as much as you did. Dad wanted it for her. They loved me despite the circumstances."

"That's amazing. They're both amazing. But I still can't quite understand why they told you. That had to be traumatic. When did they tell you?"

"When I started dating. They always suspected that it was somebody local. Dad had taken the four oldest kids with him to Dickinson. Mom stayed home with Lee. Only local people knew that. The ranch isn't on a main road. And she said the rapist seemed to know the layout of the house. Mom and Dad worried that I might end up dating my half-sister. They wanted me to know why it was especially important that I practice safe sex."

"How did you take it?"

"They made it so much easier than it might have been. They started with how much they loved me, made sure that I didn't doubt it. They explained why I needed to know. I guess I took it pretty well. But dating was pretty hard after that. I would only date girls who didn't look like me. And their dads couldn't look like me either. The idea of having sex with my sister worked better than a cold shower. All three of my steady girlfriends moved into town after I was born."

"That was a sensible precaution."

"One of the reasons Dad gave for supporting this move was so I wouldn't have to worry about the gene pool."

"Then you impregnate the woman who came with you."

The corner of his mouth turned up. "I checked. Your family moved to town when Mom was carrying me. We're safe."

"When did you check?"

He lied. "When we were getting ready to move down here. It finally seemed possible that we might actually get together."

"You *had* been planning this. I can't imagine my dad doing something like that anyhow. But I suppose a lot of people have said that about criminals. I have new respect for Nancy. She was the person who helped me most when I thought I couldn't have another baby. I was so depressed. That's when we became close friends. She understood."

"You know, I should have seen this coming. Mom never had all the tests like you did. They just figured, if God wanted her to have a baby, she would. And when they found all the kids in India and Korea needing homes, they decided that was His answer."

"But what do you mean about seeing this coming?"

He grinned. "I forgot to make my point. There was nothing wrong with Mom. And there was nothing wrong with you. You both found that out when you had a different source."

She caressed his cheek. "I wish her experience had been more like mine.

Maybe we'll talk about it some day, if she ever speaks to me again."

"Don't worry. She'll get over this. Although she'd probably get over it faster if we were married."

"Probably." She studied him. "Wait a minute. Was that a lame proposal?"

"You could think about it."

"You'd marry me?"

"Sure. It's the honorable thing to do."

"You're so sweet. I've come to terms with this, Cody. You know, I've even talked to the pastor. I messed up."

"We messed up."

"Okay. But you don't have to marry me. It's enough that you'll be a good father and help raise our baby."

"But we're still living in the same house. People will still believe we're sleeping together."

"I've talked to the pastor about that too. We're okay, Cody."

"If you change your mind, the offer stands." He smiled. "So, how'd you get your name?"

"That's easy. Dad was Karl, Mom was Leah."

"Oh. I always wondered. Your parents must have been older when they had you."

"Dad was forty and Mom thirty when they married. They tried for ten years before I came along. That's why it didn't take much to convince me that I had problems. Back to baby names. You must have been thinking about them. What did you come up with?"

"Nothing. Or maybe too many things. I can't make up my mind."

"It's early yet. Oh, feel this." She placed his hand on her abdomen.

When he felt his baby move, his eyes glistened. "I'm sorry. It's just so ..."

"Don't be sorry. Hang on to that joy. You feel so deeply. I respect that. Bill couldn't be bothered to feel Deb move. He said she was his third kid. It was no big deal anymore. I think you'd still have that sense of wonder if we had ten kids."

"I helped create that life. It takes a real cold heart not to be moved by that."

She nodded. "I'm beginning to think I was a fool to love Bill. I'm seeing him more clearly all the time. I think he married me because I was a good babysitter for his kids."

He hugged her. "Don't let it get to you. You can be grateful you didn't figure that out when he was alive. You had a reasonably happy marriage."

"Because I was blind."

"It kept you from being miserable."

"I suppose."

"I've wanted to ask for years. Now that you're seeing him more clearly, I'm going to. You were only eighteen when you got married. Did Bill seduce you?"

"It's a fair question." She pulled away. "Not sexually. He never touched me till after we were married. Never even kissed me. But, in the broadest sense of the word, yes, he seduced me. He treated me like an adult when I babysat the boys. We had long talks. He asked about my dreams."

"Bill Johnson?"

"I know. He could be charming when he wanted something. He gave me my first jumping saddle for my eighteenth birthday. My first hunter for a graduation present."

"What did your parents think of that?"

"They thought he was being pretty extravagant. But I was too thrilled to listen. Three weeks after graduation, he proposed. We were married in August."

"How soon did the verbal abuse start?"

"Not till after Deb was born. I think he knew he'd have to train me because I was so young. And I adored him, so I tried really hard to please him. Once I had a baby, I had other priorities. He didn't care much for that."

"That's probably why he didn't want you to have more. They'd take even more of your time."

"Yes. That sounds exactly like Bill's logic."

***

The new filly struggled as Cody held the cup of iodine against her navel.

"I know it stings, sweety. But it will protect you from some really bad stuff. All done."

Karlea watched him over the stall door. "Four fillies and no colts. A good year for babies."

Cody rubbed the black and white pinto, getting her used to his touch. He smiled. "You going to have a colt or a filly?"

"I feel like I'm carrying a little horse. What would you like?"

"Anything healthy, but a son would be great. I might never have another kid."

"Oh, come now! Some woman is going to snap you up."

"Sure. They're just searching for a man living with the mother of his child. If one comes looking, I should probably be leery."

"You have a point."

"So it makes perfect sense to marry you. I might get another kid. We're already living together. And you're awfully good in bed. I'd have it all."

"Then you meet your perfect woman. I won't put you in that spot."

He wiped his hands on a towel, walked to the door, and kissed her. "There's no such thing."

"True."

They left the barn, enjoying the early spring morning. He squeezed her hand.

"Don't take this wrong. After we finish foaling, I need some time to myself. I want to take Dan somewhere there are no people."

"Why would I take that wrong? You've barely had a day off since you moved here."

"You've been a little sensitive lately. I didn't want to hurt your feelings."

"Me? Sensitive? It goes with the territory. Hormones."

"I know. I read the literature."

XXV

The doctor studied Karlea's test results. "Your pregnancy is proceeding normally. You and your baby are both in good health."

"It's nice to know the tests confirm how I feel. Do you have Bill's medical records yet?"

"Yes, finally. I can tell you why you failed to conceive. Unfortunately, it's worse than I suspected."

"Something was wrong with him."

"No. Nothing. With Dr. Smith's knowledge, your husband had a vasectomy." She gasped. Cody kissed her cheek. The doctor continued. "Based on the date, you were pregnant with your daughter at the time. If Dr. Smith were alive, he'd lose his license for this."

"I'm sure it was Bill's idea. He probably didn't trust me and thought it would be a good way to catch me if I cheated on him."

"That doesn't excuse the physician. I'm sorry that I had to give you this news."

"It's okay. That was my past. My present is so much better. Bill reaped what he sowed. Dead of a heart attack at fifty-three. I don't have to mourn him anymore."

"Well, that's a much better attitude than you had the day I first saw you. Stay positive."

***

Karlea watched Cody bathing a yearling filly for a potential buyer. The filly had chosen this morning to roll in the mud. Her body, normally eighty percent white, now matched the red clay soil. After two complete washes, he turned off the hose and used a sweat scraper to squeeze the water from her coat.

Karlea sighed. "I feel useless. I could comb her tail."

"No. I don't want you near any horse's hind legs until after that baby comes. Work on her mane if it'll make you feel better."

She smiled and picked up a brush. "I thought we put such a high price on her that no one would be interested. But Bruce said he wants one of Rullah's offspring, and he saw you show Kelsey last year. Her price didn't seem to matter when he heard that they're full-brother and sister."

"He still might decide she's too expensive and put a deposit on one of the foals."

"That would be better. I'd really like to keep Cricket."

"I don't want to show this year." He let Karlea think about that while he wiped the filly with a towel to remove the marks from the scraper.

"Okay."

He paused. "That's it? You're not even going to ask for a reason?"

"You want to be home to help me with the baby."

"Yeah. Thanks for understanding." He resumed his task. "What do you think of the name Kelly?"

"We already have a Kelsey."

"Not for a horse. For our baby."

"Oh. Boy or girl?"

"Either."

"Um-m. Yes, for a girl. But for a boy, I prefer Cody."

"I won't have a junior. If you like it that much, we can use it for his middle name."

"You're making this difficult. How about Alexander?"

"Where did that come from?"

"I thought about variations of our parents's names. Your dad's Allen. Alexander has an association with horses. Alexander the Great. Alec Ramsey from the *Black Stallion* books."

He nodded. "I like it. I think she's presentable."

They heard Molly barking.

"Good thing. That must be Bruce. I'll greet him."

Cody gave Cricket a mist of coat polish. He heard Karlea call Bruce over to the stable and his surprise at her condition. They entered the stable together.

"Bruce, I'm sure you remember Cody."

"Of course." They shook hands. "Well, Cody, you show and groom. What are you anyhow, the manager here?"

Cody glanced at Karlea, who patted her belly.

"Cody does a lot of things around here."

He grinned and Bruce laughed until he cried. "O-kay. I'm not even going to try to top that comment."

***

The next day, Dotty helped Karlea shop for baby clothes. Before they finished, the wind began blowing, creating intermittent dust clouds. Dotty helped carry bags into the house. Karlea invited her to stay for coffee.

"Where's Cody today?"

Karlea smiled. "He had shopping too. Since we sold Cricket, we decided it would be a good time to buy a new baler. He'll be home in time for chores. I can't wait to show him all the things I bought."

"I'm sure he'll be *thrilled*."

"Actually, he enjoys everything about becoming a father. I can already tell he'll be a good one." She chewed her lower lip for a moment. "Dotty, I need to talk to you about something in confidence."

"You know I can keep my mouth shut."

"I appreciate that so much. But this is a big one. Do you remember me telling you that Cody's parents adopted five kids before he was born?"

"Now that you mention it, I do."

Karlea told her the circumstances of Cody's birth while Dotty gaped. Karlea concluded. "It just amazes me that they could look at something so terrible in a positive light."

Dotty shook her head. "I've met Nancy. Not one in a thousand women could find that silver lining. I would have never pegged her for having that strength."

"Over the years, I've seen it from time to time. But it always comes as a surprise." She took a deep breath. "I think Bill raped her."

Dotty's eyes widened. She sputtered. "That's a leap from where I stand. You must have more information."

"Yes. It happened after Bill's first wife died. Several people have told me that Bill drank his way through that first year."

"Still a stretch. I'm sure there were a lot of other drunks at the time."

"Be right back." Karlea returned momentarily with a manilla envelope. "I found this in the back of one of Bill's desk drawers when I was moving. When you look at it, remember that Bill never showed any sign that he liked

Cody. In my opinion, he treated him pretty badly."

Dotty dumped the envelope's contents, mostly newspaper clippings. Among them, she found Cody's high school graduation announcement and two pictures. Both Cody and Bill appeared in the pictures as part of a larger group. The clippings covered the time from Cody's birth to his completion of farrier school. It seemed that Bill had collected any mention of him.

"Oh, my God. Oh, my God. Okay, it's not a stretch."

"That's not all. This envelope made no sense at all till Cody told me about the rape. When I found it, I was busy packing. I tucked it away and forgot about it. Since then, I've been looking back to see if I missed any clues. It was Bill's idea to hire Cody to help me when he was only fourteen."

Dotty nodded. "I remember it surprised me that he did something so thoughtful."

"Out of character. And I don't know how many times I noticed that Cody and Ben walked the same. A couple of times I confused one for the other at a distance."

"Of course. Half-brothers. My God. He's a half-brother to your kids."

"Now you're getting a picture of my world. There's one more thing. Bill had only made one change to his will since Deb's birth. He paid Cody's way to shoeing school with the stipulation that a percentage of the loan would be forgiven each month he worked for me. Bill forgave that debt in his will."

"Out of character too. You've convinced me."

"But how do I tell Cody?"

"Good God! You don't."

"But he deserves to know the truth."

"Why? He only wanted to know so he could punch Bill in the mouth. Telling him won't give him that satisfaction. He may even feel frustrated by it. He already hates Bill enough for the way he treated you. Besides, if you tell him, you have to tell your kids."

Karlea bit her lip. "You don't think I could skip that part?"

"That would be a real slap in the face. Here's the truth, but you have to keep it a secret."

"Oh. You're right. Two of my three kids see their father through rose-colored glasses. Even Ben would have a tough time with this. But I just feel like Cody deserved more than having his student loan forgiven. Bill owed him more than that."

"Well." Dotty smiled. "He got more than that. He got Bill's wife. And for a few months there, he *really* enjoyed Bill's wife."

Karlea blushed. "M-m. Maybe that *was* better revenge than a punch in the mouth."

"A lot more satisfying. In my opinion, you should burn the contents of that envelope. Cody has a good life without that knowledge. Leave well enough alone."

"No. I keep it under lock and key. There's a chance he could find out some other way. If that happens, I want him to know that on some level, Bill cared about him."

"How could he find out?"

"I know the chance is remote. But, as an example, say Ben needed a kidney transplant. And neither Deb nor Gordy was a compatible donor. I'd have to tell Cody."

"I see your point. What if he asks you what you have locked away?"

"He knows about my box. He says it's none of his business."

"Okay. Add a letter explaining everything. But consider putting it in a safe deposit box instead. You don't want to take any chances."

XXVI

Cody arranged for Kevin and Jill to do chores during his three-day trail ride, telling them that Karlea would not help.

However, she joined them in the stable on the pretense of supervising. She found herself lonely without him. She also slept in his bed, taking comfort from his scent.

The second day she called Dotty for the distraction of another shopping trip. When Dotty picked her up, she studied her friend.

"You really miss him."

Karlea sighed. "Intensely."

"Are you in love?"

"Oh, *please*." She chuckled. "He's fifteen years younger than I am."

"What's that got to do with love? His age didn't matter in bed."

"It's not that. Why would he want a woman so much older?"

"That's not what I asked. How do *you* feel about *him*?"

"I don't know, Dotty. He's so much better to me than Bill ever was."

"Glad you can see that. What's not to love?"

"Oh, he's not perfect. He has a stubborn streak. And sometimes he can mull things over for months before he offers his opinion. He's sensitive. His feelings are easily hurt. And he's overprotective."

"You sound like you love every one of his faults."

"I don't mind them."

"I told you to look for a lover under your own roof. Why not a husband?"

"Oh, he'd marry me. Just being gallant, of course. But I appreciate the gesture, even if it was the lamest proposal I've ever heard. He tried to lure me by pointing out that marriage would make my pregnancy more palatable to our relatives. And, of course, he offered sex as an incentive too."

"He's still holding out on you?"

"He won't change his mind. It really bothered him."

"Well, then he's making a good offer."

"I won't tie him down like that. In ten years I'll be forty-nine and his thirty-year-old soul mate will come along. What then?"

Dotty shook her head and smiled. "I thought you two *were* soul mates."

***

The next day Karlea attended church, then worked on a special supper for Cody. He had told her to expect him early in the evening. As she removed pies from the oven, she heard Molly barking.

"Cody can't be here yet."

Seeing Dotty's car, she felt uneasy. Dotty always called before visiting. She opened the door.

"This is a surprise."

Dotty did not meet her gaze. "Karlea, try to stay calm. Hank's friend, Jay, was expecting Cody back to his ranch by noon. At 3:30, he still wasn't there."

"Jay must have misunderstood. Cody told me he wouldn't be here till about six. He doesn't need six hours to get here from down there."

"That's what he told you. Jay said he planned to come home early and surprise you."

Karlea placed her hand on her stomach. "Something's wrong."

"It could be minor, like a thrown shoe."

"Cody's a farrier. He always carries tools and nails."

"Okay, not a thrown shoe. But there are all kinds of minor things that could make him late. No reason to panic."

"No. But I'd feel better if I could do something. Is anyone doing something?"

"Jay called the forest service with a description of Dan. He and a couple of his neighbors are driving around, checking with binoculars. Hank's trying to get hold of another friend with a plane. When he does, they'll go up and look."

"It's nothing but forest down there." Karlea sank into a chair. "Can we go down to the ranch to help?"

"No. You need to take care of yourself and your baby. And we can all say some prayers."

"Of course. But I feel so helpless."

"I understand. I'll stay with you. I'll call the ranch and have them call here if they have any news."

***

When Kevin came for evening chores, Dotty told him what she knew and asked him to do the morning chores also. He agreed and offered additional assistance. She told him to pray as well. Shortly after 6:00, Kate arrived with an update.

"I took Dad to the airport. They took off at 5:30. They'll have at least a couple of hours of daylight for their search."

"That isn't long," Karlea said.

"No. But I think we're blowing this way out of proportion. This should be nothing for Cody. He told me he camped in North Dakota during the winter."

"At least a couple times a year."

"He can handle the White Mountains in late April. He knows how to take care of himself. And I've never seen a more level-headed horse than Dan."

"I know all that. That's why I think something terrible happened. It had to be something Cody couldn't handle."

"Karlea, don't think the worst. He could just be lost. This is new territory for him."

"Not Cody. He's very good in the wilderness. He might be lost for a little while, but not this long."

"I know he's okay. You're always talking about how tough he is. And I've seen it."

"That's right," Dotty said. "I agree with Kate. He knows how to take care of himself."

"I'm going home. Call me if you hear anything."

Dotty held Karlea's hand. Karlea seemed unaware of her until tears came.

"He has to be okay, Dotty."

"He is."

"He has to come home so I can tell him that I love him."

"He will, Karlea."

"Why did it take this for me to see that?"

"That doesn't matter. You know it now. You'll tell him when you see him."

"I will. Even if he doesn't feel the same, I have to tell him."

XXVII

The evening dragged. Darkness fell and still no word. Karlea stared through the window, looking for headlights in the empty driveway.

Dotty sometimes coaxed her to drink something, but she turned down food. Little conversation passed between them. Dotty hugged her often instead. At ten, she tried to convince Karlea to go to bed. She refused.

The phone rang at 10:30. Dotty answered, recognizing her brother's voice.

"Jay has him."

"They found him, Karlea. How is he?"

"I don't know much. They took him to an urgent care clinic in Springerville. A doctor's checking him out. Don't know if he's sick or hurt. But when we spotted him, he was riding. Can't be too bad."

Dotty relayed the information to Karlea, standing by her elbow. "Hank spotted Cody, riding. Jay picked him up and they have a doctor checking him."

"Thank God. How soon will we know more?"

"When can you find out more, Hank?"

"We landed at Jay's ranch. I'll take Cody's pickup and trailer up there and call when I have more to tell you. It's all back roads, so don't expect anything for a couple hours."

"He won't know more for a couple hours. Call my cell phone. I'm putting Karlea to bed and I don't want the phone to disturb her. I'll stay here."

"Okay. Talk to you later."

"Thanks. You're the best."

"I know."

Karlea scowled. "I'm not going to bed. I have to wait for Cody to call."

"Sounds like he'll be busy for a while. Don't worry. If he calls, I'll wake you."

"I can't sleep now."

"What would Cody want you to do?"

"Take care of our baby."

"You're beat, Karlea. Go to bed."

***

Karlea again slept in Cody's bed. She woke from a nightmare at 4:00 AM and turned on the lights. When she walked to the kitchen, Dotty stirred on the sofa.

"Did Hank call?"

"Yeah." She checked her watch. "They should be on their way by now. Hank couldn't leave till they unhooked the IV. Cody caught a flu bug. He couldn't keep food down from Friday evening till Saturday evening."

"Oh, my! That's terrible when you're home in your bed. It's dangerous a day's ride from civilization."

"But Cody's smart. He kept himself going by putting sugar and salt in his water. Sunday morning he somehow managed to saddle Dan and get on board. He wasn't with it enough to know where to go, so he gave Dan his head. But Dan headed home, not to Jay's ranch."

"A horse *would* come home."

"He'd been riding all day. The airplane made the difference. They called his location to Jay and his neighbors, who picked him up just before dark. The doc ran some tests and gave him an IV. He'll be fine with rest."

"I'll just be glad when he's home."

They talked for an hour. When headlights appeared in the driveway, they rushed outside. Hank climbed from the pickup and stretched.

"He's sleeping. When you wake him, don't be surprised if he's out of it. The doctor prescribed sleep and lots of it. He may be a little unsteady. Get him to bed. I'll take care of Dan."

Karlea caressed Cody's cheek and he opened his eyes.

"Karlea?"

"Let's get you to bed."

"Sounds good."

He tried to move without unbuckling his seat belt. After removing that, he slid out of the pickup, staggering with his first step. Dotty helped Karlea guide him to the house.

"We'll take him to my bedroom," Karlea said.

Dotty left to make coffee, while she helped him undress. She pulled the blankets over him. "I love you, Cody."

He yawned. "Love you."

After her initial surprise, she dismissed his words. When tired, a person automatically responded in kind. She sat with him until she heard Hank's voice. She joined them in the kitchen, where he provided more information.

"The trees were so thick, I wouldn't have spotted a black or bay horse. But I saw a flash of white through the branches. We circled back and there he was. We called Jay and kept circling."

"Thank God you have a friend with a plane."

"Yeah. We knew something was wrong as soon as we got a good look at him. He didn't even look up. He was riding like a sack of potatoes. And Dan was covering terrain that would make a mountain goat proud. We were able to stick around till Jay got to him. Said he had a death grip on the saddle horn."

"You're sure he'll be okay?"

"Yeah. The doc said he'll sleep as much as he needs to. Don't worry about that. Feed him when he wakes. Keep water by the bed. When he feels better, he'll stay awake more."

"Okay. Thank you for finding him. It means so much to me."

"You and Cody are my friends. It's the least I could do. Time to go home for some shut eye. Took a cat nap while I waited for him. Sis, can I bum a ride?"

"Absolutely."

XXVIII

Karlea snuggled up to Cody and slept all morning. When she woke, she lay there for a few minutes, savoring his hard body against hers. But she finally pried herself away to work. She arranged for Kevin and Jill to do chores until Cody told them otherwise.

Frequent checks always found him sleeping. At 3:30, she noticed a half-empty water bottle. He had been awake for a little while. Late that evening, she discovered him sitting on the edge of the bed, the empty bottle in his hand.

"How are you feeling?"

"Tired."

"Would you like more water?"

"Sure."

"Are you hungry?"

"Sure."

Karlea retrieved the sandwiches she had made earlier. He ate one before speaking again.

"Why am I in your room?"

"I wanted you close."

"Oh."

He ate and drank while she resisted the urge to touch him. He finished all the sandwiches.

"Do you need more?"

"No, thanks. I think I'll go back to bed."

He drank, then she kissed his cheek.

"Sleep all you want. I love you, Cody."

He blinked at her. "What do you mean?"

"I love you. I'm sorry it took something like this to make me see it."

He stared at her, opened his mouth, closed it, then spoke. "It's about time."

"What?"

"I've only loved you for the past four years."

"What?"

"I'm tired."

She moved to let him lay down, then wandered back to the kitchen. *He's in love with me. Four years! Even before Bill died. Cody was serious when he asked me to marry him. Why didn't he ever say anything?* Next time he woke, she intended to find out.

***

The following morning Cody rose before Karlea. When he stood, every muscle told him to go back to bed. But his brain needed to accomplish something. He would start by making coffee.

She joined him as he poured his first cup. They hugged without speaking, then took their usual places at the table. She could almost see a light go on.

"Karlea, last night, did you say what I think you said?"

"I love you."

"I love you. Will you marry me?"

"That's a little better than last night's response. Four years? Why didn't you tell me?"

"Fear."

"Why?"

"Just a minute." He left the room for several minutes. When he returned he carried the small notepad he kept in his saddle bags.

"Sorry. I couldn't find it. Out there, when I wasn't sure I'd survive, I wrote how I feel and why I couldn't say it." He took a deep breath. "'Karlea, I love you. I'm sorry I've been afraid to tell you. I thought it was safer to love you in secret. I was afraid you'd reject me and all I'd have accomplished was to ruin what we have. I still came close to saying it a few times, but something always got in the way. I didn't want an affair. But it was another way to show my love for you. That's why it hurt so much when you didn't want my baby. But I can't die without telling you how much I love you."

She wiped tears away. "I love you, Cody. You were probably right. I wasn't ready to hear that from you. I must not have been ready to see it either, because it should have been obvious. You've never denied me anything. If I had known, I wouldn't have suggested the affair. You couldn't refuse."

"Of course, I could have. But I made a calculated choice. If I was in your bed, there wouldn't be someone else there. And the chance to make love to you was just too tempting."

She smiled. "You tried to make me fall in love with you."

"Since I moved down here."

"Yes. I'll marry you."

His eyes glistened and he covered his face. She hurried to wrap her arms around him and they both let the emotion sweep over them. In a moment, he pulled her into his lap and wiped his eyes with a smile.

"Look at me, bawling like a kid."

"Remember, I like you to show your feelings. You've been under a terrible strain. I'm so sorry I hurt you. I love you, Cody."

"It's all okay now. I can finally say how I feel." He caressed her belly. "How soon can we get married? I want you to be my wife."

"We just need to get a license."

"Great. Is a quick marriage okay? Maybe you want to invite our families."

"No! I'd rather they find out afterward."

"My sentiments exactly. So how easy is it to get a marriage license?"

"We probably just need our birth certificates."

He whistled. "Mom and Dad still have that. If I ask them for it, they'll want to know why I need it."

"You could tell them you want to get a passport."

"I guess I'd rather not lie to them."

"I understand." She frowned. "We're only 350 miles from Vegas."

"How soon can we go?"

"You should have a couple more days rest before our wedding night."

His grin faded. "Are you sure it's still okay? I don't want to hurt our baby."

"Absolutely. We just need to be a little conservative. Should we ask Dotty and Hank to be our witnesses?"

"Better than a couple strangers."

"I'll call Dotty."

"I'll do chores."

"No, you won't! Kevin and Jill are doing chores until you feel better."

"Okay. But I'll do them tomorrow morning."

***

Cody did chores the next morning, then slept most of the day. Karlea used the time to call Ben on his cell phone.

"Are you really busy?"

"No. Just on my way to Dickinson for a meeting."

"By yourself?"

"Yeah. What's up?"

"Ben, I need you to do something for me, no questions asked."

He chuckled. "Is it legal?"

"Yes."

"Okay."

"I'd like you to get a DNA test."

Silence filled the line. "O-kay. I know I promised I wouldn't ask any questions. You can choose not to answer this one. Do you ever plan to tell me why?"

"Honestly, I don't know. I'm not sure what I'll do with the information after I get it."

"Okay. Anything for you, Mom."

"Thanks, Ben. I love you."

She disconnected and gazed out the window. *Thank God for Ben. He's a great son. I could never have asked Deb or Gordy to do that with no explanation.* When her baby kicked, she rubbed her belly. She really had no idea what she intended to do with the test results beyond comparing them to Cody's. She had collected hairs from his pillow earlier.

Maybe I just want it for ammunition if Deb gets really obnoxious when she finds out about Cody and me. She'll probably think he's just after my money. It would be nice to tell her that he deserves what I inherited from Bill as much as she does.

She smiled, thinking about the look on Deb's face if she heard that news. Deb had some of her father's feeling of superiority. It might not hurt her to be brought down a notch.

"Enough premature gloating. Back to work."

When Cody woke, she barred him from the evening duties, encountering little resistance. He left the house only to supervise the help. When he returned, he inhaled.

"If the smell of beef on the grill doesn't make me hungry, I'd better see a doctor."

She smiled. "You've eaten plenty the past couple days."

"I'll be myself in no time." He hugged her. "You know, there are a lot of things we haven't discussed."

"I know. You are going from an employee to my husband. I can't just keep paying you a salary."

"Why not?"

"Because it won't be my money. It will be our money. Bill never put my name on the ranch account. If I wanted something, I had to ask him for money. I hated that. I won't do it to you."

"You already have my name on the farm account. I don't see that anything has to change."

"Your name may be on there, but you won't spend a dime without informing me. I trust you. You aren't frivolous. You won't buy anything we don't need. Consult me about the big ticket items."

"Okay. I'll try to remember that."

"All the new foals will be registered in both our names. And I want to get your name put on this place."

"That'll be really complicated. And it won't be free. You don't have to do that."

She kissed him. "Yes, I do. Not just because I'm marrying you. You've earned it. You've dedicated your life to my horses. You've helped make a name for this place. I couldn't have done any of this without you. You made my dreams, your dreams. You acted like my husband years before you started getting any of the benefits."

"I loved you the only way I could—by working hard."

"I love you for that. But are you sure you want to go through with this? When you're forty, I'll be fifty-five."

"I am *so* sure about this. You're a beautiful woman. But that isn't why I love you. The reasons I love you will still be here when you're ninety."

"But when I'm ninety-five, you'll have second thoughts."

She grinned and he rolled his eyes.

"No. When you're ninety-one."

"I love you."

"I love you. Do you want more kids?"

"Let's see how this one goes. Ideally, I'd like another one. Deb grew up like an only child because the boys were so much older. Maybe that's why she's so possessive of me. But, will I feel the same after going through labor? Or after a couple months of sleepless nights?"

"Fair enough. If you want more, you won't have to talk me into it."

XXIX

Dotty, Hank, and Kate picked them up early Thursday morning. Kate teased Karlea.

"Now I can say that I've slept with your husband."

Karlea kissed Cody's neck. "Only one night. You only got a little taste of his talents. He's very creative."

He grinned, blushing. Kate laughed.

"No wonder you're marrying him. You must be *so* satisfied."

"Satisfied and pregnant. Just two of the many things he can do that Bill couldn't. Or wouldn't. My second marriage is already better than my first."

He kissed her for such a long time that Kate, in the third seat of the SUV, feigned prying them apart.

"Let her breath! That baby needs oxygen."

They both laughed, but he scolded her. "Be quiet back there."

"Leave them alone, Kate," Dotty said. "Cody has waited a long time for this."

Kate left them alone and they both dozed during part of the trip. They woke near the outskirts of Las Vegas.

Dotty had chosen a conservative, out-of-the way chapel. No drive-up weddings or Elvis impersonators. Cody climbed from the vehicle and helped Karlea out.

She squinted at the bright sunlight, then her eyes widened. "Cody?"

"What is it?"

Her eyes rolled back. He caught her as she fell.

"Karlea!"

She regained consciousness before he could do more. He sat her on the floor of the SUV and she blinked at him.

"What happened?"

"You fainted."

"Oh. Never done that before. I felt funny."

Dotty handed her a bottle of water. "Drink this. Did you have breakfast this morning?"

"Sure."

"I'll get some juice out of my cooler. Drink it, just in case."

Cody studied Karlea, his brow furrowed. "You should see a doctor."

"Can't it wait till after our wedding?"

"You want to faint again during the wedding?"

"Cody's right," Hank said. "Better to be safe than sorry."

Dotty handed her the juice. "I'll go in and tell them why you can't make your appointment. There's an urgent care clinic not far from here."

***

Cody found one empty chair in the waiting room. He directed Karlea to it, then procured the paperwork. He stood beside her for an hour before a nurse called her name. The nurse asked a few questions, took her blood pressure, and listened to the baby's heart. Another half-hour passed before a lab technician collected blood. And almost another hour before they saw a female doctor.

"Good afternoon, Ms. Johnson. How are you feeling now?"

"Pretty good. Just a little concerned."

She held a stethoscope to Karlea's belly. "Your baby sounds fine. Have you ever fainted before?"

"No."

"Have you ever been diagnosed with hypoglycemia?"

"No."

"You drank 20 ounces of orange juice about two hours before your lab work. Is that correct?"

"That sounds right."

"Your blood sugar was on the low side of normal. In my opinion, you have pregnancy-induced hypoglycemia. Divide your food into several smaller meals and see your doctor when you get home. Give a copy of this lab work to your doctor. Any questions?"

"Is it okay to go ahead with our wedding?"

"Eat first. Take it easy on your honeymoon. Don't exert yourself on an empty stomach."

Karlea blushed. "Yes, ma'am."

They walked to the casino next door, where the rest of their party had waited. Cody explained doctor's orders and Dotty called the chapel from the restaurant. They could get married in an hour.

As they entered the chapel, Hank voiced a question. "Do you have rings?"

Karlea held up her hands. "Our engagement was too short and my hands are too swollen. We'll get rings later."

"I'm giving her my class ring today," Cody said.

Hank laughed. "You know that just shouts your age difference?"

"I know. And yesterday she found the first picture taken of us together. I was about a year old. But, you know what? That's my baby she's carrying. I'm old enough."

She kissed his neck. "You certainly are. I like having a husband who can keep up with me. And when I'm ninety, I'll *really* appreciate having a younger husband."

He chuckled and they proceeded with the ceremony.

Kate acted as wedding photographer. When the minister told Cody to kiss the bride, he followed it with a long hug and a whispered word.

"Finally."

"I love you, Cody."

"I love you, Karlea Pfeiffer."

***

Cody watched Karlea unbutton his shirt. "You know I'm not interested in sex right now."

She licked her lips and smiled, unbuckling his belt. "Have I ever failed to get you interested? We'll start with a shower."

"Okay."

He let her finish, then undressed her. He placed both hands on her very pregnant belly, his eyes glistening. She caressed his cheek and he tried to explain.

"It's just not the same with clothes."

"Keep that sense of wonder."

She held off on foreplay until he led her to the shower. It took longer than usual to gain his interest. She dried him before they returned to the bedroom.

"I did this just over a year ago."

"What? Oh, dried me off. After the ice storm. I still don't remember it. But that was the first night we slept together."

"It's so much more fun with sex."

He chuckled. "No arguments here."

With great care, he lowered her to the bed. After more intense foreplay, he prepared to finish. The baby kicked his stomach. He jumped back, eyes wide.

"Did I hurt him?"

She smiled. "He's just reacting to how excited I am."

"Are you sure? I don't want to put you into premature labor."

"Don't worry about it. We'll be fine."

"But I *am* worried about it."

She patted the bed beside her. "Lay down. I told you. Just be conservative."

"But how conservative? I don't want to take any chances."

"Our marriage won't be official till we make love."

"Oh. I suppose not. But I'm less interested than I was before."

"I guess I need to give you the detailed lesson." She trailed her fingers across his body. "There will be a practical test at the end of this class."

He gasped. "I was always a good student."

"Good. You just need to overcome your test anxiety."

***

A few days after their wedding, Karlea saw her doctor in Show Low. He agreed with the diagnosis. Eating frequent meals had eliminated the problem.

Afterward, they shopped for rings, using her old wedding ring to find the proper size.

Life at home changed little. They corrected people who called asking for Mrs. Johnson. Cody became more attentive as her pregnancy progressed.

She smiled when he helped her with a routine task. "I won't break."

"Humor me."

"Okay. Would you like some loving?"

"Hadn't thought about it. Would you?"

"Yes."

"I guess I should do something about that or you'll look elsewhere."

"Not likely. Are you still worried about putting me into labor?"

"No. I'm just contented. I don't think much about sex. I'm happy having my wife and our baby."

"Do you have everything you ever wanted?"

"Nobody has that. But I have all the important things I ever wanted. It can't get any better than this."

"Sure it can. When our baby actually comes. But we still have to figure out how to tell our families."

"I'm ready to call Mom and Dad. I'll just ask them to sit down before I say it."

"But I'm afraid Deb will never speak to me again."

He hugged her. "That's out of our hands."

"I know. Let's not talk about it now. We have better things to do."

He grinned. "Okay. I'll help you procrastinate a while longer."

XXX

The router whined, spraying sawdust which stuck to Cody's bare chest. Karlea had insisted that he change the sign at the end of the driveway to "Karlea and Cody Pfeiffer." He stopped, raising his goggles to wipe sawdust and sweat from his face.

Molly began barking, warning him that someone had entered the yard. He walked to the open garage door, trying unsuccessfully to brush sawdust from his chest. When he saw the car, he froze.

"Oh, Lord."

He continued toward the front door as fast as he could without appearing to hurry. He gave a casual wave, just to show his lack of concern.

Then he opened the door and yelled. "Karlea! Deb's here!"

Better to have a little warning than none at all. He faced Deb as she climbed from the car.

"Hello. This is a surprise."

"I know. We were down to Albuquerque to see Ted's folks. I just came for the day."

"Where's Darla?"

"She's teething. She's such a grouch, I left her there. Are you going to let me in?"

"Sure."

He stepped aside, then followed her in. Karlea, looking pale, stood behind a high-backed chair.

"This is certainly a surprise."

"That's what Cody said. You going to come hug me?"

Karlea hesitated before stepping into the open.

Deb's jaw dropped. "Geez, Mom, you've put on weight."

Karlea looked from Deb to Cody. He joined her, taking her hand. She spoke as gently as she could.

"Deb, I'm not fat. I'm pregnant."

"Huh? Oh, come on, Mom. You know that's impossible."

"That's what I said when the doctor told me. But there's a baby in here."

Deb stared at her belly. Then frowned. Then scowled. Her eyes turned to Cody, filled with hate. She screamed several expletives at him. "You didn't waste any time taking advantage of my mother!"

Karlea's brow furrowed. "Deb, that's my husband you're talking to."

Deb sputtered, then screamed. "How could you be so stupid! He's only after your money!"

Karlea's eyes filled with tears.

Cody took charge. "Deb, shut up! You've already said too much. If you can't show more respect, get out."

She made an enraged sound and called him another filthy name. "You have things just the way you wanted them! Well, I hope you two are very happy together!"

She slammed the door behind her. Cody wrapped his arms around his sobbing wife. Karlea shook her head.

"I should have called her."

"It wouldn't have made any difference."

"How can she be so selfish?"

"She'll get over it, but it'll probably take a while. Under the best of circumstances, this would've been a shock for her."

"I suppose. Would you come snuggle with me?"

"Sure. But I'd better take a shower first. If I get this sawdust in the bed, we'll both itch."

***

Cody still lay in bed with Karlea when the phone rang. He checked caller ID before answering. "Hello, Ben."

"This wasn't exactly what I had in mind when I asked you to take care of Mom."

Cody heard the smile in his voice. "You didn't give me specific instructions."

"I'll have to remember that next time. When Deb called, I thought she was joking. How the heck did that happen?"

"The usual way."

"I know. Stupid question. But I understood it was impossible."

"Given what we know now, it was inevitable. Are you ready to hear something unpleasant about your father?"

Silence filled the line. "Go ahead."

"It was only impossible because he had a vasectomy."

More silence. Cody gave him all the time he needed.

Ben sighed. "I wish I could say that I'm shocked. But I can barely manage surprise. Dad was a selfish man. I heard him say that he didn't even want Deb. But he figured if Mom didn't have a baby, he'd never hear the end of it."

"He had the vasectomy while she was still pregnant."

"And had Doc tell her that she had too many problems to have more kids. Selfish and cruel. I wonder if he treated my mother as bad. I'm ashamed to be his son."

"I think Karlea needs to hear you say that. I'll let you talk to her."

Karlea cried and said "Thank you" several times before handing the phone back to Cody.

Ben chuckled. "You know, I'm going to tell my kids to call you grandpa."

"Great."

"I really wasn't planning to have a little brother or sister at this stage of my life."

"I doubt Deb was either."

"I'll work on her. She's acting like a spoiled brat. If Mom had gotten knocked up on a one night stand, she probably would've taken it better. She just doesn't like you."

"I'll say. Did she tell Gordy too?"

"No. I convinced her to let me do that."

"How will he take it?"

"He knows my sense of humor. He won't believe me. He's more like Dad than I am. But we both knew that Mom was the one who really loved us. He'll take it better than Deb. I'll call tomorrow evening with a report."

"Thanks."

"Next time I see your dad, I'm calling him grampaw."

"Geez, wait till tomorrow. We haven't told them yet."

"Okay. You got till tomorrow morning."

***

"Hi, Mom," Cody said. "How's everything?"

"Good. Done with spring's work. Too early for cultivating."

"Is Dad home?"

"Want to talk to him?"

"Put him on the other phone."

"Allen, get on the other phone! This sounds important."

"It is." He heard the phone pick up. "You should both be sitting down."

"What's wrong?" Nancy asked.

"Nothing. Are you sitting?"

"Yes. Yes. What is it?"

"I'm sorry you have to find out like this. I got married." He heard a loud clatter as someone—probably his mother—dropped the phone. "Dad, is Mom okay?"

A short pause. "She's still upright. Was this a whirlwind romance, or have you been keeping something from us?"

Cody heard his mother retrieve the phone. "I kept it from you. I didn't tell anyone. Not even her. I've loved her for years."

He let them absorb that. Finally, Allen caught the implication. "My Lord, you married Karlea!"

"Allen, don't be silly. Karlea's fifteen years older than Cody."

"Mom. Dad's right."

"Karlea?"

"We're shocked," Allen said. "But we want you to be happy."

"We are, Dad."

"But, Cody," Nancy protested. "You'll never have kids."

"I fell in love with Karlea knowing that. I love her so much that it didn't matter. But ... we found out it was a lie. We're expecting."

A very long silence. Again, Allen caught on. "You didn't say a mistake. You said a lie."

"Bill and Dr. Smith lied to her. Bill didn't want more kids, so he had a vasectomy."

"That dirty S O B!"

"Allen! I didn't like the man either, but that's no excuse for such language."

"Sorry, honey. Karlea deserved better. He probably thought she'd cheat on him. Figured she'd get pregnant if she did."

"Yes, she deserved better. Now she has it. We're happy for both of you, Cody. She wanted a baby for so many years. When is she due?"

Cody took a deep breath. "In less than a month."

A short silence, then Nancy blurted. "You've been married *that* long?"

"Nancy, think before you open your mouth."

"Oh. Well. At least you're married now."

"Thanks, Mom. It's not the way I wanted it to happen. I'm not proud of myself. But I love Karlea and I'm really happy that I could give her a baby."

"I want to come down. I'll come and help after the baby is born."

"We'll probably appreciate that. I've never done this and it's been twenty years for Karlea."

"I'll send your mom," Allen said. "I'll be busy in the hay field by then. I'll have to settle for pictures till this winter."

***

Karlea answered the phone when Ben called.

"How'd Gordy take it?"

Ben chuckled. "Gordy will be okay with this. I decided to give it to him in pieces. The marriage announcement only bothered him because he didn't get invited. When I told him you married Cody, he said something that had crossed my mind. I won't repeat it."

Karlea smiled. "Was it about sex?"

"Yeah. He figures that's the main reason you married Cody."

"He's wrong. It was only the third or fourth reason."

"I'll tell him. Then we got to the baby. He *would not* believe me. I had to make him call Deb. When he finally called me back, he said he'd help me change her attitude."

"She's so jealous of Cody. She must see this as a real slap in the face."

"I suppose. But, Mom, that's her problem. This isn't about her. Now that I've had time to look back, I can see that Cody's loved you for years. We probably would've noticed if he'd been closer to your age."

"Maybe I would have noticed too."

"Have you told his folks?"

"Yes. You're free to torment Allen."

"Looking forward to it."

***

After a lengthy discussion, Cody convinced Karlea not to answer the phone if Deb called. He wanted to spare her the stress if Deb's attitude had not changed.

More than a week after Deb's visit, he took the call. Deb hung up, only to call back a few minutes later. He tried using her name.

"Hello, Deb."

Another click. And another call a half-hour later. He tried a different approach. "She's not answering the phone."

"Let me talk to her!"

"Not till I hear what you want to say."

"This is just what I thought! You're driving a wedge between us!"

"You don't need my help for that. You're driving the wedge. Your mom loves you. If you can show her the respect she deserves, you can talk to her."

She called him another filthy name and disconnected. He turned to Karlea.

"Where did she get that dirty mouth?"

She sighed. "I guess I can blame her father for that too."

"Yeah. She sounds like him."

"I guess she hasn't accepted our marriage yet."

"Good guess."

XXXI

"Cody," Karlea said. "I think we should go to the hospital."

He froze with his hand on the dresser drawer. "The baby?"

"I think so."

"You think?"

"It's been a long time. But I'm pretty sure this is labor."

"Okay ... I'm staying calm. I'll get your overnight bag. Wait here."

"I'll put my shoes on."

"Me too." He removed her pre-packed bag from the closet and strolled to the kitchen for his boots before returning. "Ready to go?"

"Yes. Are you?"

"Sure."

She grinned. "You look great. But a shirt might be appropriate."

He looked down. "So I'm not calm."

He pulled on a T-shirt and helped her to the pickup. He managed not to exceed the speed limit on the twenty minute drive to Show Low. At the hospital, they waited for some time while Karlea's discomfort increased.

"Are you sure now?" he asked.

"Oh, yeah. This is labor."

"Should I hurry somebody?"

"No. This will probably take hours."

"Can I do anything?"

"You already are. I love you, Cody."

"I love you."

A nurse interrupted their kiss. After a short wait in an exam room, a doctor pronounced her in labor and they proceeded to the maternity ward. Cody barely left her side. He studied the fetal monitor.

"Is it normal for his heart to beat that fast?"

Karlea smiled and caressed his cheek. "Yes."

"How are you?"

"My back's killing me. Not bad otherwise."

"Is that normal?"

"Yes."

"Would it help if I rubbed it?"

She fought tears. "You're so sweet. It can't hurt."

"I love you, Karlea. I got you into this condition. It's the least I can do."

***

When Karlea's doctor checked again twelve hours after her arrival, he decided he needed to stay. Cody held her hand and coached her. After one long contraction, she gazed at him.

"This may be your only child."

"I know."

"There's one consolation."

"Besides the baby?"

"Yeah. At least I had fun getting pregnant."

She smiled, then grimaced with another contraction. Cody did not notice her vice-like grip on his hand while he watched the birth of his son. The doctor placed the big boy in Karlea's arms.

Her smile returned. "Oh, he's beautiful."

Cody felt elated and relieved, but would not have described his son as "beautiful." *He's a wrinkled, slimy mess.* Handsome or not, he loved his child.

"I love you, Alex. I love you, Karlea."

"I love you, Cody. Isn't he perfect."

"He's pretty special. And he's big!"

"I noticed."

"I love you. So it's okay that I gave you a baby?"

"Oh, yes! You knew what I wanted before I did."

He kissed her. "I'll get out of the way while they finish up. I need to make some phone calls. And I'm sure Dotty's still in the waiting room. I'll be back in a little while."

***

Alex demanded attention. When he woke, he only stopped crying long enough to eat. Sometimes walking with him helped. Cody logged miles around the house. He did as much as he could to let Karlea rest, even bringing Alex to her at night. He became adept at placing his son where he could nurse.

All other work suffered. With school out, Kevin and Jill worked full-time, freeing him to stay in the house. That usually involved walking with Alex.

Dotty tried to help. But Alex screamed when she held him. She admitted that she had never been good with kids, volunteering to cook and clean instead. Cody took the offer.

Everyone looked forward to Nancy's arrival. Dotty drove to Phoenix to pick her up on the day Alex turned three weeks old.

When Nancy saw their condition, she ordered Cody and Karlea to take a nap, getting no arguments. Karlea woke when she smelled supper. She found Nancy in the kitchen, holding Alex and stirring something on the stove.

"You're a marvel."

"Just a grandma. Glad you're up. He'll be hungry soon."

"I'll take him. This was so much easier when I was eighteen."

"It's not your age. I remember Deb was an easy baby. Alex is his father's son."

"Cody was a fussy baby?"

"Don't you remember? The first time you babysat, you had to let one of the older kids hold him. He screamed whenever you got near him."

Karlea smiled as she nursed Alex. "I'd forgotten that. He kind of insisted that I try to forget. He's made that easy. Nancy, we've shared so much since I found out I was pregnant." She hesitated. "He told me how you got pregnant."

Nancy froze. "He did? Yes, I suppose that's something you should know. At least he's married now. He doesn't have to worry about falling in love with his sister."

"We even discussed that. I only bring it up because I wanted to tell you what an amazing person you are. You handled it so well."

"Only because I had Allen. When I found out I was pregnant, I was in such denial. I wanted to believe it was his baby. He wanted me to be happy. But he wouldn't let me lie to myself. After I accepted the truth, I couldn't stand to be alone in the evening. I often smelled the cigarettes and alcohol on the rapist's breath."

"You never saw him?"

"No. He put a pillowcase over my head. He never said a word. After he left, I took a shower. That's why we never told the authorities. All I could have told them was that he was a smoker and drinker. I'd destroyed any other evidence."

"Did you ever get over the flashbacks?"

"Long ago. I think they ended the first time I felt Cody move. Some people might wonder how I could love a child made that way. How Allen could love him. We love five adopted kids. How could we not love Cody?"

"I understand. Do you ever wonder who it was?"

"Any time I think about it. But when I do, I remind myself what a great kid he gave me. If he was somebody local, I like to imagine him seeing Cody grow up and wishing he could have a relationship with him."

Karlea bit her lip and changed the subject. "I'm sorry I seduced your son."

Nancy paused, then smiled. "Somehow, I don't think that's what happened. While Cody was still in high school, he used to vent to me about how Bill treated you. I think he was already falling in love with you. And I know you weren't seducing him then."

"He said he was twenty when he fell in love with me."

"That's just when he realized it. Men take a while to catch on. Now we know why he stopped dating. I always thought it was my fault."

"He dedicated his life to me. He showed his love the only way he dared. I always appreciated him. I knew I had a very special right hand man. But I just couldn't see that he loved me."

"You couldn't stop thinking of him as a kid."

"He forced me to."

"When?"

"After he moved here. Even then, I was blind. Or naive. He asked me to let him kiss me."

Nancy turned from the stove. "And you didn't figure out what he was up to?"

"He said it would prove that I didn't think of him as a kid anymore. It seemed like an odd request. But like I said, I was naive. And after he kissed me, I wasn't thinking very clearly. Your son's really good at that."

Nancy blushed. "Oh, my. Did *he* seduce *you?*"

"No. He worried about that too. I told Dotty that I felt like going wild. But I didn't trust any man enough. She reminded me that I had a very handsome, trustworthy man living under my roof. When I approached him about it, I made it clear that he could refuse with no hard feelings. I didn't know that he couldn't refuse me."

"You didn't force him, Karlea. He always had a choice. He has just been choosing to please you for a very long time."

"I'll have to remember that. I don't want to ask too much of him."

"I think he's learned to be honest with you."

Karlea nodded. "You're right. After that scare down in the national forest, I don't think he hides anything from me."

"What scare?" Karlea grimaced as Cody entered the kitchen. "Cody, what happened in the national forest?"

He shot Karlea a withering glance. "No big deal. I came down with the flu while I was out trail riding. I wasn't in any danger, just pretty miserable. I knew what to do."

"You could have died."

"Mom. This is exactly why I didn't tell you. Give me credit. I'm no dummy. I can take care of myself."

Nancy fluttered a hand, then rubbed her face. "Of course, you can. I'm sorry."

"And I probably won't camp alone anymore. I have a family now."

"Good," Nancy and Karlea said.

XXXII

For the next three nights, Nancy insisted that Karlea fill bottles for Alex, allowing her to keep him in her room. The new parents managed six straight hours of sleep before the bottles ran out.

During the day Nancy cooked and cleaned and took her turn caring for Alex. By the fourth day of her visit, Cody and Karlea no longer felt exhausted.

When Nancy sent them off for another nap, he smiled at his wife. "I'm not tired."

"Neither am I."

"Are you feeling up to some loving?"

"I am. But I'm not really interested."

"I can get you interested. But we don't have to. I can wait."

"But you don't want to wait."

"No."

"We can do this. No wild sex. Very gentle."

"I can do that." He unbuttoned her blouse. "I suppose you want me to use protection."

"You'd better, if you expect more than a kiss!"

"Okay. But I kind of like it without."

"You'll take it any way you can get it."

"True. If we're not going to have more kids, I should do something permanent. Those things aren't foolproof."

"They're not?"

"You didn't know that?"

"I've never had to worry about birth control. I could still get pregnant?"

"There's a very small chance. Does this change your mind?"

"That'd be pretty selfish. But it could effect how much I enjoy this. The only time I worried about getting pregnant was when I wanted to."

"I want you to enjoy sex. I *should* do something foolproof."

"Don't do that yet. We may still want another baby."

He froze, eyes wide. "After all those hours of labor and the sleepless nights?"

"What can I say? I like babies."

"I used to. But Alex is trying really hard to change my mind."

"He's getting better."

"Only because Mom's here."

"Maybe." She rubbed his arms. "Now, do you plan to tease me into bed, or are we going to talk all afternoon?"

He kissed her neck.

***

"Nancy, sit down," Karlea said. "I have something to tell you."

They took chairs at the kitchen table. Karlea opened her mouth twice, but no words came. She fingered the manilla envelope.

Nancy squinted. "This must be really serious."

Karlea nodded. "And very hard to say. I ... know who raped you."

Color drained from Nancy's face. Her hands trembled. Then her jaw tightened and she let her breath out. "Tell me."

"Bill."

"Bill?" Nancy nodded. "Yes. He's one of a handful of guys I suspected. I don't think you'd tell me if you didn't have proof."

Karlea extracted a sheet from the envelope. "These are DNA test results from Cody and Ben. The important information is the sentence on the bottom."

Nancy read it aloud. "The probability that these two individuals have a different father is 14,500 to 1."

"I'm sorry."

A corner of Nancy's mouth turned up. "Why? You didn't even know Bill Johnson when he raped me. You have nothing to be sorry for. You've actually given me some peace. It always bothered me that it might have been someone I considered a friend. I *never* liked that jerk." She pursed her lips. "Does Cody know? Does Ben?"

"No. I need your advice on that. Should I tell them? Will it be easier for Cody if he doesn't know?"

"Easier, yes. Better, no. Anything is better than wondering. Now I know that Bill Johnson got what he deserved in the end. He thought he got away with it. The Lord just took his time punishing him."

"There's something else you should know." She tapped the envelope.

"You got your wish. These are newspaper clippings of every accomplishment Cody had before Bill died. I found them in Bill's desk. He knew what he was missing."

"Oh-h." A tear ran down Nancy's cheek. "Wanting revenge isn't very Christian. But that envelope is better than spitting in Bill Johnson's face. I'll help you tell Cody about it."

"Maybe that will make the news easier for him."

At that moment, Cody entered the house. He looked from one to the other. "What's wrong?"

Nancy patted the table. "Sit down." He pulled out a chair. Nancy handed him the test results. "Read the bottom line."

Cody read it, then glanced at the entire page. "Who are these two?"

Nancy caressed his cheek. "You're one of them." He stiffened. "The other is Ben."

He stood, nearly toppling the chair, then ran both hands through his hair. He swore. "That S O B! And I can't even hit him. I can't even spit on his grave without driving a couple days." His eyes glistened. "I *really* wanted to hit him. I've been thinking about that since you told me you were raped."

"I know. This is better."

"Better? How?"

"Cody," Karlea said. "You got his wife."

He stared. Then he fought a smile before letting it come. "When you put it that way, it is better." He gave Karlea a long kiss. "Talk about irony. Or poetic justice. I'm not sure which. I feel much better." He sat again. "Mom, how do you feel?"

"Better. I don't have to wonder anymore."

He turned serious. "Yeah. That feels good. How did you figure it out?"

"Karlea did."

"How?"

Karlea explained about the connection she had made to the contents of the envelope. "Somehow, in his own sick way, Bill cared about you. But that didn't make him admit to his crime."

His jaw tightened. "One of the few thoughtful things we thought he did for you wasn't thoughtful at all. He hired me so he could see more of me." He shook his head. "You said that was Ben's DNA. Have you told him?"

"No. Do you think we should?"

He ran a hand through his hair. "I don't know. It gave Mom and me some closure. Do you think there's any point in telling them that their father was a rapist? Would that just be vindictive?"

"I don't know. It has to be your decision. I won't ask you to keep quiet about it."

"If it was just Deb, I could be *real* vindictive. After all the years she looked down her nose at me." His eyes widened. "My God, I kissed my sister. With tongue. No wonder it was so disgusting."

Karlea squeezed his hand. "It was disgusting because you couldn't stand her."

"That too." He took a moment. "He didn't think she was too good for me. He threatened me so I wouldn't have sex with my sister."

"Of course. That's how Bill would deal with the problem."

"He didn't know it was just business." He let his breath out. "Anyhow, I'd tell Deb in a heartbeat. But I don't want to hurt Ben. He's my friend. He's already heard enough revelations about his father. I guess I don't dislike Gordy that much either."

"We'll do whatever you want. I'll give you one more piece of information though. I asked Ben to do the DNA test and send me the results, no questions asked. What do you want me to do if he asks?"

"If he asks, let me tell him. I'll make it as easy as I can."

XXXIII

Cody checked the caller ID before answering the phone.

"Hello, Deb."

A short silence preceded the sound of Deb's sigh. "I've accepted that Mom loves you. Ben believes that you love her. I'm not ready to buy that, but I'm willing to wait and see."

"That's mighty generous of you."

Her silence conveyed her reaction. *I don't care. If I try to appease her, she'll turn on me later.*

Finally, she continued. "I shouldn't have taken my dislike for you out on her."

"Are you willing to apologize to her?"

"Yes. I was in shock. I might have reacted differently under better circumstances."

"I won't let you keep hurting my wife. If you blow this, it will be a *long* time before I let you talk to her again."

Another silence. "I get it! You're a controlling bastard."

"Only where you're concerned."

"You'll never be the man my father was."

"Thank God for that." She hung up. Cody smiled at his empty office. "Guess that was the wrong thing to say."

She called back a few minutes later. He dispensed with the greeting.

"You don't like me and I don't like you. I didn't like your father either. Don't try to insult me by comparing me to him."

"I get it. I want to talk to Mom."

"Here are my conditions. You can call me anything you like. But not when she can hear you. Tell her you intend to wait and see. If you weren't lying to me, it will be the truth. I'll listen in on any conversations you have with her till I'm satisfied that you're sincere. Can you live with that?"

"If I want a relationship with my mom, I guess I'll have to."

"Good choice. Just a minute." He took the phone to the bedroom where Karlea had just put Alex down for a nap. "It's Deb. She says she's ready to apologize."

"You believe her?"

"I think so. Take the other phone. I told her I'll be listening. If she gets out of line, we hang up."

She nodded. He sat on the bed and held her hand. She picked up the phone.

"Hello, Deb."

"Hi, Mom. I'm sorry I went off like I did. It was just such a shock. Maybe if you'd called me I would have handled it better."

"Do you really think so, Deb? Can you imagine any way you could have heard the news that I married Cody that would have led to a different reaction?"

Silence. Then Deb cleared her throat. "Maybe if I'd had time to get used to the idea. Like if you'd told me that you were dating. I mean, for me, he went from your hired man to your husband in an instant."

"Yes. I know that was very hard for you. I'm sorry it happened that way. And that's all my responsibility. Cody wanted to tell everyone, but I was afraid. I felt like some kind of cougar, taking advantage of a younger man. And I felt foolish because he suggested using protection and I saw no reason for it."

"So, you had an affair before you married him?"

"I just wanted to be irresponsible for once. I didn't know that he loved me. I thought we were just having fun." She squeezed Cody's hand. "He would do *anything* for me."

Another silence. "Okay. Maybe Ben's right. I'm willing to wait and see. I'll stay away for a while. But I'll call sometimes."

"I'll look forward to that. Deb, you have a little brother."

"Ben told me. He says he looks just like I did as a baby."

"Yes, he does."

"Send me a picture."

"I will. I love you, Deb."

"Love you, Mom. Take care."

When Karlea disconnected, she began crying.

Cody held her. "It's a start."

She nodded. "I really thought she'd never speak to me again."

"I guess she learned from you when to admit she's wrong. She sure didn't learn it from Bill."

"I must have done something right."

***

For the remainder of Nancy's two week stay, they traded off nights with Alex. By the time she returned home, he slept four hours between feedings. Cody and Karlea would be able to get enough sleep even without an assistant.

Satisfied that Karlea no longer needed his help day and night, Cody put more hours into riding, starting the young horses under saddle.

When Ben called to say that he would visit, they looked forward to it. He even saved them a trip to the airport by renting a car.

From his vantage point on horseback, Cody saw a car turn in the driveway. Not Ben. There were two occupants. He rode to the gate. The driver looked like Ben. As it approached, he recognized both occupants.

"Oh, Lord!" He dismounted and handed the reins to Kevin. "Groom her for me. You two finish up chores. We have company."

He failed to notice Kevin's puzzled expression as he hurried toward the house. Ben stood beside the car, stretching while Deb remained in the passenger seat, glaring at Cody. Ben extended his hand, and Cody shook it.

"This isn't funny, Ben."

"No. I spent the last day talking until my mouth was dry. I told her not to come if she couldn't be civil to everyone."

"She doesn't look civil."

Ben shrugged. "She came."

"Okay. She knows my conditions. I can take whatever she dishes out. But I *won't* let her hurt my wife."

"Neither will I."

"Good. Is she coming?"

"We'll just let her sit there."

They wandered toward the house without inciting Deb to move. Inside the door, Karlea hugged Ben.

"Hi, Mom."

"Thanks for coming. Did you have to kidnap her?"

"No. Ted offered to throw her in the trunk, but I didn't want her along if she couldn't be nice. I think she's just reminding herself of that now."

"She can stay there till she's ready. I won't go to her. We're having this problem because I spent too many years making allowances for her moods. I don't have time for that anymore."

"Way to go, Mom! Where's that little brother of mine?"

Karlea and Cody exchanged glances.

"Sleeping. And we *do not* disturb him. He should be awake soon."

"Can I at least have a look at him?"

"Sure."

Cody had barely taken his eyes off Ben's car. "I'll keep an eye on her."

Ben chuckled. "She's not dangerous, you know."

"Just being a good host."

"Liar."

As they left the room, Deb opened the car door, but stayed in the vehicle. Five minutes later, Karlea and a chuckling Ben returned.

"Cody, it's probably not what you want to hear, but I think he looks just like Deb."

Cody shrugged, glancing at Karlea. "I've resigned myself to that. We looked at Deb's baby pictures while Mom was here."

"It's kind of funny though. I always thought Deb looked as much like Dad as she did Mom." Cody's eyes darted to Karlea, who tensed. Ben looked from one to the other. "What did I say?"

"Nothing."

"That's no better lie then your crack about being a good host."

"Okay." Cody sighed. "No more lies. But it isn't going to be easy to hear."

"I'm a big boy."

"Be right back." Cody checked to see that Deb had not moved before retrieving the test results. "Do you remember when Karlea asked you for a DNA test?"

"Yeah. Now I find out why?"

"Yes."

Cody handed him the sheet. Ben studied it for a few seconds.

"When I got my results, I tried to figure out what all these little marks mean, this top one's me." He gazed a little longer. "Is the bottom one Deb or Gordy?"

"Neither. I'm sorry, Ben. It's me."

Ben gaped. He looked from Cody to the results, and back again.

"Allen isn't your biological father?"

"No. They never told anyone. Mom was raped."

"Oh, my God. Dad? Dad did that?"

"I'm sorry. It was the year after your mom died. He was drinking at the time."

"Yeah. He drank his way through that year. He'd drink all evening, then tell us how sorry he was in the morning. We were just little kids. We didn't know what was going on." He hesitated, a far off look in his eyes.

"What is it?"

"One morning was different. I came downstairs before Gordy got up. Found Dad crying in the kitchen. He kept saying, 'What have I done?' I was so scared. I just hugged him. He didn't drink for a couple days and he never left the house. Then he went back to the bottle. That must have been when it happened. It was another six months before he straightened himself out."

"That would be the right time frame. We weren't going to tell you. Didn't think you needed to hear more bad news about your dad. I just don't have much of a poker face."

"I would have had to ask about that test sooner or later. I was way too curious. Did Dad know?"

"Yes."

Karlea elaborated. "I found an envelope in Bill's desk. Everything was about Cody. It didn't make any sense till Cody told me how he was conceived."

Cody glanced out the window and found Deb standing beside the car. "What about Deb and Gordy? Do you want to tell them?"

"Save it. Use it on Deb if she doesn't get an attitude adjustment. That should get her over thinking she's better than you are, once and for all. If you have to tell her, I'll break it to Gordy." Ben shook his head. "So, *you're* my new little brother. I guess that explains why Alex looks so much like Deb."

"Yeah. Here she comes."

Cody opened the door for her without saying a word. She entered, tight-lipped. While the silence dragged on, he wrapped his arms around Karlea. Even Ben, who hated awkward silences, kept his mouth shut.

Deb finally spoke. "Hi, Mom. Just remembering the last time I was here."

"I love you, Deb. You always hated surprises."

"That didn't qualify as a surprise. But I love you, Mom. I just want you to be happy."

"I am happy. And for the first time in a long time, my happiness doesn't depend on your approval. I'd love to have it. But I don't need it."

Deb looked near tears. "I'm just afraid he'll hurt you. I don't want you to get hurt."

"Cody takes such good care of me. You're the only one who's hurt me."

Deb's lip quivered. "Look how I found out. Why couldn't you tell me?"

"I couldn't even tell Ben, and I thought he'd take it well. I was afraid of your temper."

Deb blinked. "Afraid of me?"

"I was afraid of your disapproval. Afraid this would drive us apart. I couldn't think of a way to tell you that wouldn't lead to this. Was there a way?"

Deb wiped tears twice before answering. "I guess not. I can't get over how I feel about him."

"Well, if you want a relationship with me, you'll have to. He's not my hired man anymore. He's my husband. Cody left his home for me. He's not going anywhere. We're a package deal. If you *force* me to choose between you and him, I'll choose him."

Deb stared, then nodded. "I understand. Like I said, I'm willing to wait and see. But, Cody, I'm warning you. If you ever leave her, cheat on her, or do anything to justify my dislike for you, I'll make you pay."

The corner of his mouth turned up. "It won't happen. But remember the same warning. I won't let you hurt her."

"That's fair."

Alex wailed. Cody kissed Karlea's cheek.

"I'll get him. Hug your daughter."

When he returned with Alex, the hug had not ended.

Deb broke away. "Let me look at him. I always wanted a little sister. But a little brother is okay too." Alex scowled at her. "He looks like you, Mom."

"He must." She met Cody's gaze. "Because he looks just like you did at this age. And you never know. You might get that little sister yet. Are you two planning to stay a while?"

"If we're welcome."

"Of course. If you keep this attitude."

"I'll do my best."

XXXIV

Everyone noticed the tense atmosphere, though Cody had to admit that Deb seemed to be trying. He did the same. But he hurried in from chores, wanting to be there to protect Karlea from potential attacks. She assured him that Deb had behaved during his absence.

The next morning, Deb found him alone in the kitchen. He leaned against the counter, facing her.

"It's just you and me. Say what you like."

"Maybe you love her. I just know that this is pretty sweet for you. You go from a stable hand to having your name on the front gate. Did you con her into making you co-owner too?"

"I didn't con her into anything. But, yeah, she thinks I've *earned* co-owner status. I've worked hard for her."

"Trying to work your way into her bed. Even before Dad died. Ben told me. He thinks it's just fine that you had your eye on her while Dad was still alive. I think you're an ingrate. Dad gave you that job. And you repay him by taking his wife."

He bit his lip and counted to ten before responding. "You make it sound like she cheated on him. I didn't touch her till she bought this place. She was a widow."

"Don't lie to me. I saw you holding her. More than once."

Cody's eyes narrowed. "I held her lots of times. She needed hugs every time he yelled at her or put her down. He treated *her* like a hired hand. Even worse, he treated her like a real lousy boss would treat a hired hand."

"Dad was tough on everyone."

"I'm sure that was very comforting to her."

"Why do you hate my dad so much?"

He clenched his fists. "Isn't how he treated your mom enough?"

"He never hit her. Lots of women have it worse."

This time biting his lip and counting to ten could not stop him. He fairly spat his reply. "He raped my mother."

Deb stared, then laughed without humor. "Give me a break. You're lower than I thought. He can't defend himself. If you repeat that, I'll sue you for slander."

Cody took the offensive. "It's only slander if it's a lie. I'm your half-brother."

Her eyes widened. Silence dragged on. She shook her head, as if clearing it. "That's a lie."

"No, it's not," Ben said, stepping into the room.

"Ben, you can't believe this."

"I believe the DNA tests. Cody and I have the same father. That makes him your half-brother too."

"But ... Dad wouldn't do that."

"You didn't know him then, Deb. He was drunk all the time. You always saw him at his best. That makes this harder for you. You have to take him off that pedestal you put him on. He had a lot of flaws. He treated Mom like crap. He knew how much she wanted another baby. But instead of telling her he had a vasectomy, he got Doc to tell her she had all kinds of problems. You don't do that to someone you love. And he put her down, a lot."

Tears ran down Deb's cheeks. Cody watched her, feeling unsympathetic. But he kept silent, letting Ben deliver the blows.

Ben continued. "Cody loves Mom. He deserves to be a full partner in this place because Dad owed it to him. Dad knew that Cody was his son. But what did he do for him? Gave him a job and sent him to horseshoing school. And he made him work that off. *Big deal.* You, me, and Gordy got a lot more than that."

"Are you sure he knew?"

"We'll show you the envelope he kept. Everything Cody ever did. He knew."

For the first time, she looked at Cody. "He always told me bad things about you. When we had that arrangement for my prom, he told me that you weren't good enough for me." She took a ragged breath. "He didn't really mean it. He just didn't want anything to happen between us. I'm sorry. I believed him."

Cody's chest felt tight. "He was your father. Of course, you believed him. *He* was the reason I could never do anything right in your eyes. I don't know if you could have ever gotten past that."

"I was trying. But you're probably right. I'm sorry. For everything. How long has Mom known about this?"

"She figured it out not long before we got married. My folks had never told anyone outside the family that Mom was raped. I told Karlea after we found out we were expecting."

"She really loves you."

"And I really love her."

"Can I give you a hug?"

"I'd like that."

With the hug in progress, Karlea entered carrying Alex. She looked around, wide-eyed. "What happened?"

"Deb knows the truth," Ben said.

"Oh-h. Are you okay?"

Deb released Cody. "I feel like I've been beat up. I guess Cody and Ben had to knock some sense into me."

"Your dad had you brainwashed. Sorry to be so blunt."

"No. If I think of it that way, it will probably be easier to forgive myself. I've treated Cody like crap."

"I forgive you," Cody said.

She hugged him again. "You're a better person than I am."

"Your mom's right. You *were* brainwashed. You're not a bad person. I'm happy to have you as a sister." He grinned. "And step-daughter."

"Oh, my God." She smiled. "How do I explain this to Darla? To anybody? She has two new uncles. One is younger than she is. Oh, and he's also her cousin."

"You think you got problems," Ben said. "I have to explain a step-dad younger than me. Or, here's a good one, my brother married my mom."

"I think," Cody said, taking Alex from Karlea. "That we shouldn't tell anyone outside the family. I think we'll get tired of explaining it. If Bill were alive I'd want to tell the world, so everyone would know the kind of man he really was. But I don't want what he did to reflect on his family."

Karlea wrapped her arms around him. "That's very thoughtful."

Deb nodded.

Ben agreed. "I appreciate that. It's bad enough, learning all this stuff about Dad. I've been feeling like I need to apologize for him."

"You had no control over what he did," Cody said.

"I know. Still, I feel like someone needs to. At least to your parents."

"My parents are so okay, Ben. They made the best of what happened." He kissed Karlea. "And I got the best thing Bill ever had. What goes around, comes around."

###

Made in the USA
Middletown, DE
12 August 2024

58985591R00106